MERIDIAN

Going To Ground

MERIDIAN™

Going To Ground

features Chapters 8 - 14
of the ongoing series
MERIDIAN

CHAPTER 8
Barbara Kesel
Mike Wieringo
Rob Stull
Paul Mounts

CHAPTERS 9-10
Barbara Kesel
Steve McNiven
Jordi Ensign
Morry Hollowell

CHAPTERS 11-12
Barbara Kesel
Steve McNiven
Tom Simmons
Morry Hollowell

CHAPTER 13
Barbara Kesel
Derec Aucoin
Jason Lambert

CHAPTER 14
Barbara Kesel
Steve McNiven
Tom Simmons
Morry Hollowell

CHRONICLES 3
Barbara Kesel
George Pérez
Mike Perkins
Laura Martin

LETTERED BY
Dave Lanphear & Troy Peteri

CrossGeneration Comics **Oldsmar, Florida**

MERIDIAN • CHAPTER EIGHT

Far away...

on the world of Demetria, explosions rocked the surface and gigantic boulders shot into the sky and stayed there. Settlers established great city-states on these ore-buoyant islands, using floating ships to move trade goods between them. One of these islands is Meridian, home of shipbuilders and Sephie, the 16-year-old daughter of Minister Turos. Sephie's life has been spent being groomed to take over as ruler of Meridian when her father retires.

But all that changes when a mysterious force gives Turos and Ilahn the Sigil, a link to power. Ilahn gains the power of decay. Sephie's father dies, his sigil transfers to her, and she finds she has the power of renewal.

Ilahn, Sephie's uncle, whisks Sephie to Cadador, the island he rules, but she runs away after discovering how evil he is. His soldiers pursue her, knocking her off her ship, and she falls.

Ilahn believes her dead, but Sephie has survived and is in Akasia, a struggling surface city famous for its beautiful dyes which rests atop a toxic swamp. There she saves a small boy from a monster that attacks through the decaying sections of the city's structures, discovering her powers are more formidable than she thought. In thanks for her kind treatment by Akasia, Sephie extends her power through the city, transforming it back to a healthy state. For her good deed, Sephie is captured – the Minister of that city considers Sephie too valuable to allow her to leave – and put to work in the dye factories, where she discovers the terrible secret of Akasia's success: children run the factories.

Meanwhile, Cadadorian soldiers have invaded Meridian, and most of that island's inhabitants have abandoned their home. The refugees are hiding in Ring City, a bookbinding cooperative of linked smaller islands whose streets are dotted with Cadadorian soldiers watching for them.

Sephie's friend Jad Takarty has followed her to Cadador to tell her where the rest of the Meridianites have gone, but finds out he is too late and Sephie has fallen to her death. Devastated, Jad nearly follows her.

In Cadador, Ilahn plots the takeover of Meridian and mourns the loss of Sephie, daughter of the woman he secretly loved. He is comforted by the attractive presence of his ambitious new protegé, Reesha Teramu, and perplexed by the enigmatic hints of the Muse of Giatan. Then word comes from Akasia that Sephie lives, and Ilahn is awed by the potential of the power they share...

The MUSE

Far away on Meridian, there I was, studying systems of commerce and exchange....
...all fairly easy to understand, because there are general rules that almost always apply...
I studied furiously. I wanted to be as good a minister for Meridian as my papa...
...but I was studying something else, too --
-- all the confusion and changes of my OWN system.
SEPHIE...
JAD?
Not as easy to understand...
...but, still, there are rules that apply...

...and both kinds of systems are difficult to master.
SEPHIE...
WAKE UP, SEPHIE...
WHA--!
EEE!
SORRY, SEPHIE...
...BUT YOU'RE NEXT IN LINE!
THE OTHERS CAN'T GO TO WORK UNLESS YOU DO!
Work!
Yesterday I was the toast of Akasia.
Today, just another laborer at the dye factory after being betrayed and shackled with chains--a problem my power to heal couldn't fix.
Still, there's a way out of every tight spot.

But how could I leave if it meant leaving all the other children in this place?
Akasia had certainly found an INNOVATIVE way to ensure profitability for their factory...
I had no idea anyplace so inhumane existed.
But I was also FASCINATED by the fact that it did.
Even in CADADOR, the lowliest workers are treated as people, not slaves.
THIS'LL BE YOUR WORK STATION.
THE OTHERS WILL INSTRUCT YOU IN YOUR DUTIES.
GET TO WORK--THE SOONER YOU START, THE SOONER YOU EARN YOUR CITIZENSHIP.
CITIZENSHIP HAS TO BE EARNED?
ONLY IF YOU WEREN'T BORN IN AKASIA--IT'S FAIR.
HERE, TAKE THESE, AND LOOK BEHIND YOU.

Was this the way business really worked? Was Meridian the exception, rather than the rule?
YOU CATCH.
WHEN THE BOLTS COME OFF THE BELT, FOLD 'EM TEN-HIGH TO A CART.
WATCH IT--IT'S *HOT*.
KEEP YOUR GLOVES ON--YOU MAY BE SOME SORTA SPECIAL, BUT THAT DOESN'T MEAN YOU GET OUTTA YOUR SHARE'A THE WORK!
Polite is polite, but I was NOT a citizen-to-be of Akasia! I was the Minister of Meridian!
All that was between me and Meridian was one lousy chain!
But, just as before, nothing happened.
I just can't destroy.
Which meant I had to be patient... SOME opportunity would show up!
I hoped.
And gagged.

Maybe the smell is what blinded me to the very obvious solution...
My power didn't affect the iron shackles...
...but the shackles were attached to the wood...
...and I'd healed all the wood in Akasia. My power worked on the WOOD!
So if only...
...I could bring a miracle to life...
...then I could...
...I WOULD be...
KRANGK
KRAK

FREE!
Although I was still burdened by a little reminder...
...nothing a few ship's knots wouldn't bind...
...into a trouble to be unknotted later.
My immediate problem was how to take as many children as possible with me...
...especially since my little escape hadn't inspired open rebellion.
WHAT ARE YOU DOING?

I'M LEAVING!
AND I WANT YOU ALL TO LEAVE WITH ME!
YOU'RE SLAVES HERE -- COME WITH ME TO MERIDIAN!
NO?
BUT-- WHY?
THERE'S MONSTERS OUTSIDE!
THEY FEED US HERE, AND WE HAVE A SAFE PLACE TO LIVE UNTIL WE BECOME CITIZENS.
THAT'S MORE THAN MOST OF US HAD BEFORE...
REALLY?
WELL, I HAVE A PLACE FOR YOU TO LIVE, TOO, AND WHEN I GET BACK UP THERE, I'LL BE BACK TO FIX THIS PLACE UP OR TAKE YOU THERE!
I PROMISE--
YOU!
NO MORE TALKING!
--I WON'T FORGET YOU!
KLANGK

AKASIA...
WHAT A WRETCHED LITTLE CITY.
WELCOME TO AKASIA, MINISTER ILAHN.
I TRUST THINGS IN CADADOR ARE WELL?
MADAME MINISTER, MIGHT I COMPLIMENT YOU ON YOUR GOOD JUDGMENT IN SENDING A MESSAGE TO ME SO QUICKLY.
SIMPLE COURTESY -- I TRY TO MAINTAIN GOOD RELATIONS WITH AKASIA'S TRADING PARTNERS.
HMPFH.
PARTNERS. MORE PROPERLY BENEFACTORS.
NOW TAKE ME TO MY NIECE IMMEDIATELY!

WE'RE PROUD TO HAVE YOU YOURSELF COME TO AKASIA, MINISTER ILAHN.
IT'S RARE TO HAVE THE OPPORTUNITY TO SHOW OFF OUR COLORS TO SUCH AN IMPORTANT GUEST.
AND YOU NEEDN'T WAIT FOR A CARRIAGE. THERE ISN'T ONE.
WE DON'T USE FLOATING SEATS LIKE YOU SKY CITY PEOPLE. OUR OWN LEGS WORK WELL ENOUGH.
PLEASE, COME ALONG.
WALK?
LIKE A *PEASANT*?
BOSCAU, WE MUST GET SEPHIE AND RETURN TO CIVILIZATION AS QUICKLY AS POSSIBLE.
IT'S NOT FAR!

THIS HAS GONE FAR ENOUGH.
HIDING US FROM THE CADADORIAN SOLDIERS IS PUTTING TOO MUCH STRAIN ON THE PEOPLE OF RING CITY...

SO NOW WE HAVE TO MAKE A CHOICE.
THE VOTE DOESN'T HAVE TO BE UNANIMOUS-- EACH ONE OF US MUST BE GUIDED BY HIS OR HER OWN MORAL LODESTONE.

THOSE OF US WHO WANT TO REMAIN HERE IN RING CITY WILL HAVE TO GIVE UP THEIR TIES TO MERIDIAN AND ASSIMILATE INTO THE CITY.
THOSE WHO WANT TO RETAIN OUR SEPARATE ALLEGIANCE WILL HAVE TO MOVE ON TO NEW TERRITORY.

JON?

"YES, HASTIAN?"

THE CHOICE MIGHT NOT BE OURS -- THERE'S CADADORS HEADED OUR WAY!
KEEP CALM.
WE'RE IN THE MINISTRY. THEY WON'T VIOLATE ITS DOORS WITHOUT CAUSE.
MIRA!
MOVE AWAY --
"-- THEY SEEM TO FEEL THEY HAVE CAUSE."

KRAAK
WHUMP

WHICH WOULD MEAN CAPTURING US FIRST!
KREK

REMEMBER, WE ESCAPED YOU ON MERIDIAN!
WHUMP

CAPTURE?
FEABIE, ARE THEY GOING TO PUT US IN CAGES?

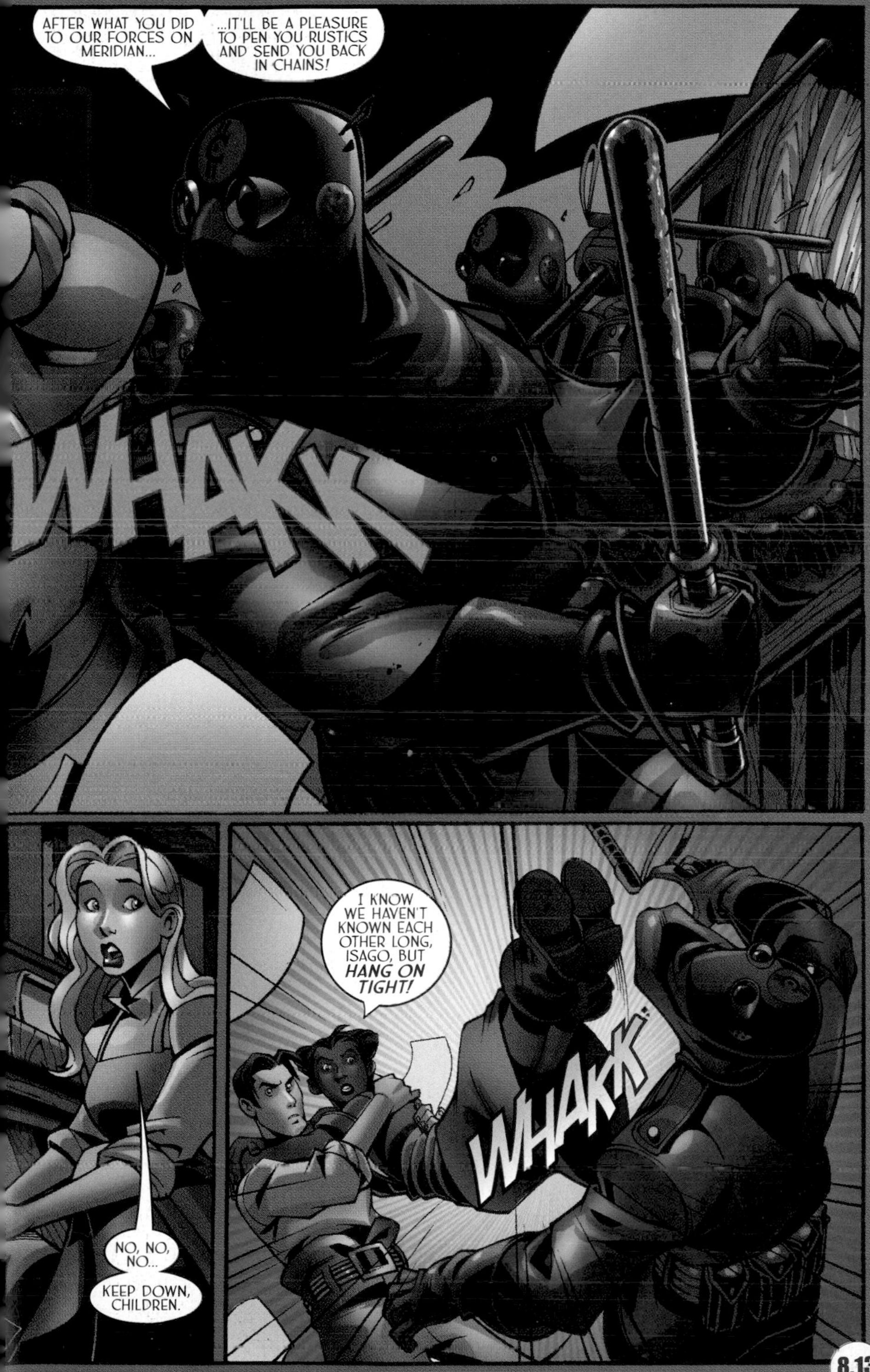

AFTER WHAT YOU DID TO OUR FORCES ON MERIDIAN...
...IT'LL BE A PLEASURE TO PEN YOU RUSTICS AND SEND YOU BACK IN CHAINS!
WHAKK

YOU STAY AWAY FROM THEM!
CLANGK

KREKAKK

FLOOMP

YOU BROUGHT THIS ON YOURSELF --
KLUMPF

--IT'S BAD LUCK TO BREAK FAITH WITH ANOTHER CITY'S MINISTRY!
WHUDD

WHEW!
THOUGHT IT LOOKED LIKE YOU MERIDIANITES COULD USE A LITTLE HELP FROM US, JON.
STRANGE WAY OF STAYING NEUTRAL YOU HAVE THERE, ODWIN.
I'M...OVERWHELMED.
YOU KNOW ILAHN WILL TAKE IT OUT ON RING CITY.
THAT'S PROBABLY TRUE...
...BUT SOMETIMES YOU JUST HAVE TO DO THE RIGHT THING AND DAMN THE CONSEQUENCES.
THERE'S NO MATTER OF CHOICE LEFT NOW, MIRA. WE HAVE TO MOVE ON.
TRUE, AND IF WE LEAVE SOON, WE CAN TAKE THE BLAME WITH US.

LEFT CADADOR?
LOROSI!
WHAT DO YOU MEAN, HE'S LEFT CADADOR?
MINISTER ILAHN HAS BEEN CALLED AWAY ON IMPORTANT BUSINESS. I'M AFRAID I CANNOT DIVULGE ITS NATURE.
LOROSI, I THOUGHT WE TWO HAD AN UNDER-STANDING...
WE DO.
I UNDERSTAND WHAT YOU WANT FROM THE MINISTER, AND I CANNOT HELP PROVIDE IT IF HE IS NOT HERE.
GOOD DAY, M'LADY.
HUH!
HIS FUTURE IS NO LONGER AS SECURE AS HE IMAGINES.

THE FUTURE IS NEVER A SECURE THING.

HMM?

OLD WOMAN...
DID YOU SAY SOMETHING TO ME?

I COULD SAY SOMETHING OF WHAT THE EYES HAVE SEEN...
...BUT IT WOULD REQUIRE ONE TO LISTEN.

I'M LISTENING.
SO, TELL ME...
...WHAT HAVE THOSE UNUSUAL OLD EYES SEEN?

ONCE DID A WOMAN CIRCLE THE WORLD FOR POWER.
ONCE WAS A DOOR OPENED TO HER.
ONCE WAS IT CLOSED.
SOON IT WILL OPEN AGAIN...
...OFFERING BOTH POWER AND PRICE.

Oh, POOR SEPHIE...
...FALLING ALL ALONE...
I HOPE YOUR END WAS QUICK...
AND PAINLESS.
AND I WISH I'D HAD THE CHANCE TO TELL YOU...
...TELL YOU...
...BUT I DIDN'T...
...AND NOW I HAVE TO TELL THE OTHERS YOU'RE NEVER COMING HOME.

Home!
Freedom was SO close...
To get away, I planned to commit my first crime and steal one of Akasia's ships.
I told myself that this was justified and that I'd send a new ship back from Meridian in exchange.
But it still didn't feel right.
Neither did seeing a CADADORIAN ship in Akasia's port!
Did Uncle Ilahn send it?
Did he know I was there?

Would he ever know if I died right here?
Not that I would, even with the heavy chain dragging me down... I had my strange power to save me.
This force... it could heal, it could PUSH...
...but it wouldn't BREAK...
...or was that just me that couldn't or wouldn't destroy?
Maybe it wasn't the power at all.

So there I was, alive, free, and on my way.
Ilahn's soldiers, Maraya's guards--
--no one could stop me.
I wasn't going back. Not to Akasia's dye factory, not to Ilahn's estate...
...and maybe...

...not even to Meridian.

MERIDIAN • CHAPTER NINE

The Celanaug evolved in the blighted regions surrounding Akasia. It's a carnivorous monster that thrives in the toxic runoff that surrounds the city.
Every so often, an Akasian is lost to a Celanaug.
I'd learned to respect its power and size during my detour in Akasia...
...so I could understand why children chained in the dye factories would choose to stay prisoners and avoid a possible encounter.
I couldn't even THINK about how afraid I was.
But NOTHING was going to get between me and Meridian...
...which meant I had to keep one step ahead of the monster.

Except there wasn't just ONE Celanaug.
That's what I got for running away from my troubles...
...MORE.

Suddenly, the power to HEAL didn't seem very powerful.
Or useful.

Papa never let me back away from a problem.
"The best way to meet it is head on," he'd say.
"Face it down..."
"...make it a crisis solved and forgotten BEFORE it turns into a monster."
I doubt he ever envisioned a problem THIS monstrous, though...

Or that I'd be racing for my life--
--on the SURFACE!--
--weighted down by the symbol of my capture.
Which I boldly put to use...
...only half-certain that any damage that made it through my makeshift armor could be healed by my power...
GRAAAUREEEEECH
...but the links were made of tougher stuff than the Celanaug.
Although...
...maybe I wasn't.
I needed a way to escape before fear stopped me dead..
Whatever it was I'd done to make myself hover over the toxins before...
...I reached inside and tried to find it now.

THIS CHIT-CHAT IS ALL VERY CHARMING, MINISTER MARAYA...
...BUT LET'S DISPENSE WITH THE UNNECESSARY NICETIES.
YOU SAID YOU HAVE MY NIECE HERE IN AKASIA.
SO FAR, YOU HAVE FAILED TO PRODUCE HER.
THERE'S BEEN A SLIGHT DELAY IN...
...WE HAVEN'T BEEN...
...I DID WHAT I THOUGHT BEST, BUT...
Oh, I CAN'T LIE.
MINISTER ILAHN...
...WE'VE... LOST HER.
LOST.

OH, I UNDERSTAND!
YOU FOUND YOURSELF WITH A SURFEIT OF TRADE GOODS AND NEEDED TO DRAW DOWN A SHIP!
SO YOU TOOK ADVANTAGE OF AN OLD MAN'S BEREAVEMENT TO OFFER HIM FALSE HOPE!
NO, I DID NOT!
SEPHIE WAS HERE AND SHE WAS BEING HELD AT THE FACTORY UNTIL SHE TOOK IT UPON HERSELF TO HEAD OUT INTO THE BLIGHTED LANDS ALONE!
BUT YOU WANT TO SEE ME TAKE ADVANTAGE? THEN JUST WATCH WHAT I'LL MAKE CADADOR PAY FOR YOUR SAFE RETURN!
YOU'RE HOLDING ME HOSTAGE.
THEN IT APPEARS I'VE MADE AN ERROR IN BRINGING ONLY A SMALL GUARD STAFF TO ACCOMPANY ME...
BUT PERHAPS MY MISSTEP...
...IS MERELY FATE IN DISGUISE...

...PRESENTING AN OPPORTUNITY FOR ME TO *TEACH* YOU WHAT IT MEANS TO CROSS CADADOR.
KRAKA-T

OOM

Being from the sky cities and not the surface, I wasn't familiar with explosions.
KATHOOM
HUH?
The phenomenon distracted me long enough...
WHAT WAS THAT?
...for my curiosity to do what my questing couldn't...
...and give me the sky.
...although I WAS still anchored to reality.

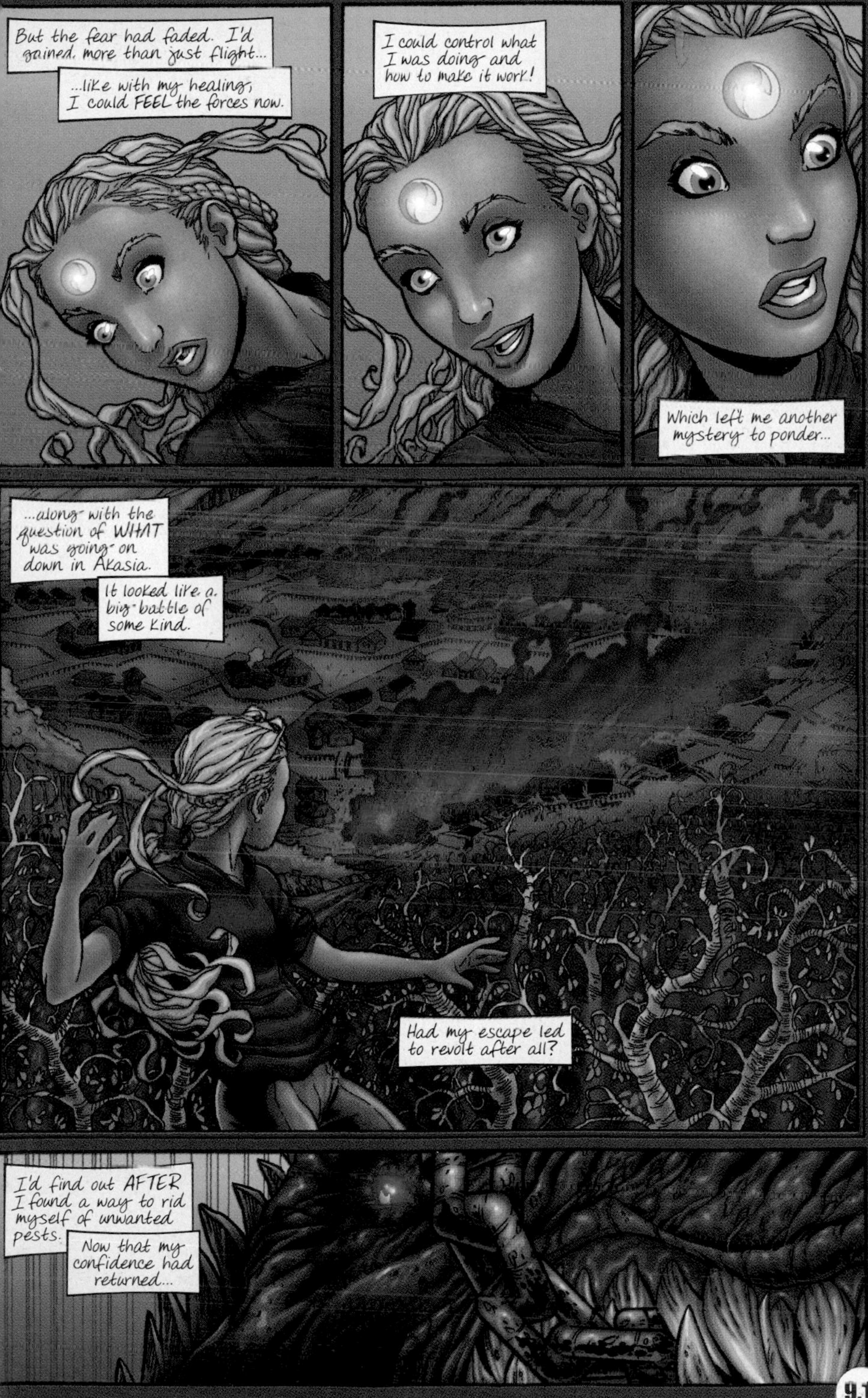

...along with the question of WHAT was going on down in Akasia.

It looked like a big battle of some kind.

Had my escape led to revolt after all?

...I was certain I'd be back to Meridian and my friends soon!
HEY!
THERE HE IS!
FINALLY!
COMING THROUGH!
PARDON ME!

ZOUKA, CAN I TALK TO YOU?
ALWAYS, FEABIE.
REMIND EVERYONE TO STAY CALM. WE'RE GOING TO GET NOTICED IF EVERYTHING'S NOT PERFECTLY ORDINARY.
AND LET ME KNOW WHEN THE LAST IS STOWED. WE WANT TO BE AWAY FROM RING CITY BY SUNSET.
NO, NOT ALWAYS.
SOMETIMES YOU'RE JUST NOT THERE TO FINISH MY THOUGHTS.
ZOUKA, THINGS JUST HAVEN'T BEEN THE SAME BETWEEN US SINCE YOU MET THAT BOY!
FEABIE...
...IT'S GOING TO GET EVEN MORE DIFFERENT.
I'M GOING TO STAY HERE WITH ISAGO.
I'M OLD ENOUGH NOW.
NO!
OH, I DON'T MEAN DON'T, BUT DO YOU HAVE TO?
I'VE BEEN THINKING ABOUT THAT...
...AND I THINK I'D LIKE TO START A WHOLE NEW LIFE LIVING IN A WHOLE NEW PLACE WITH YOU!
HEY!
HUFF
JAD'S BACK!

JAD?
WHERE, LOUWEL?
'ROUND THE RING A WAYS!
FOLLOW ME!
JAD!
HI, JAD!
...FEABIE...
...ZOUKA...
AND WHY ARE *YOU* SO TIRED?
Oh! THE LONG VOYAGE FROM CADADOR WITH JUST YOU AND SEPHIE...
...WHERE IS SHE?
SEPHIE'S... NOT COMING WITH US.
JUST BECAUSE WE LEFT MERIDIAN?
HUH!
CADADOR'S SPOILED THAT GIRL!
NO, FEABIE, I MEAN NOT EVER COMING BACK.
SHE'S...
...SHE'S...
...DEAD.
NOOO!

OH, JAD!
THAT'S SO AWFUL!
WHAT *HAPPENED?*
SHE'S FROM MERIDIAN, YET...
...SHE FELL FROM A SHIP, FEAB.
SHE WAS COMING BACK TO US AND SHE *FELL.*
"FEABIE...WITHOUT SEPHIE...THERE'S NO REASON NOW NOT TO JUST...MOVE ON."
"WE'RE *ALL* STARTING OVER, JAD. WE'RE HEADING FOR A BRAND NEW ISLAND WE CAN TAME AND MAKE INTO OUR NEW HOME...
"...SO YOU CRY ALL YOU NEED TO. YOU'RE STRONG AND YOU'LL SURVIVE THIS...
"...*WE'LL* SURVIVE THIS."

MARAYA, PUT ASIDE YOUR PRIDE AND LISTEN.
YOU'LL NEVER BE MORE THAN A MINOR MINISTER OF A FAILING SURFACE CITY IF YOU DON'T LEARN FROM YOUR MISTAKES.
FOR INSTANCE, POWER CAN BE TAKEN BY FORCE, BUT YOU MUST BE CERTAIN YOU DO HAVE THE POSITION OF GREATER RELATIVE STRENGTH.
IF YOU DO NOT, YOU ASSURE YOUR OWN DESTRUCTION.
AAAH!
I'M DISAPPOINTED IN YOU, MARAYA. YOU'D BEEN SURPRISINGLY SUCCESSFUL IN YOUR MANAGEMENT OF AKASIA.
I'D EVEN HAD MY EYE ON YOU.

I'D CONSIDERED YOU SOMEONE TO WATCH CLOSELY, THE RARE COMBINATION OF INTELLECT AND PERSONAL DYNAMISM.
A POSSIBLE STUDENT, IN FACT.
YOUR CURRENT ACTIONS, HOWEVER, BELIE THE INTELLIGENCE I'D ASSUMED OF YOU.
NOW I DON'T THINK I CARE TO HELP YOU AT ALL.
Oh, NO.
NO.
NO!
YES.
YOU GAMBLED WITH YOUR CITY'S PROSPECTS.
NOW AKASIA WILL HAVE TO PAY THE PRICE OF BAD BUSINESS.

Papa described negotiation as the art of balancing FORCE with RESPONSIBILITY.
People, left to their own, sometimes need a little push to get going.
The trick is to balance between PUSH and SHOVE.
Could papa have ever dreamed...
...how I'd apply his teachings?
The same feeling of push that kept me aloft...
...let me herd the Celanaugs far away from Akasia.
I thought of pushing them off a cliff, but I couldn't bring myself to just kill them --
-- all life has its place --
-- but I COULD keep them far away from me and farther from the children of Akasia!

Although SOME Akasians deserved to be eaten for what they did to me and those other kids!
PFFT
That task done, I was ready to head home.
My responsibility was to Meridian...
...I'd leave Akasia to solve its own battles.
I glowed with the realization that I could just FLY home...
...followed by a chilling worry--what if flying is like swimming? What if I got halfway home...
...and got tired?
As much as I wanted to bolt upward, my responsibility kept me anchored...
...to my original plan, to be a thief...

...not knowing that I wasn't going to be able to carry it out.

LET'S SEE HOW YOU ACCOMPLISH TRADE WITHOUT SHIPS!

NOO!
Uncle Ilahn hadn't sent a ship after me...
...he'd come himself.
And I wasn't the only one of us two to discover there was MORE power to the sigil.
Those lovely ships, months of our hard labor, destroyed in seconds!
Tears kept me from seeing the worst of the destruction.
Being jailed, nearly smothered, almost eaten, and now watching Uncle Ilahn destroy my escape...
...it was all just too much.
I knew I wasn't strong enough to go directly against Ilahn yet...
...I needed help.
And it wouldn't be coming from Akasia.
Not now.
And it wasn't waiting in Meridian.
So I'd just have to find help somewhere else.

MERIDIAN • CHAPTER TEN

We're shipbuilders, the people of Meridian. We take the raw buoyant timber and fashion it into skyships.
We view our work as more than just labor -- doing it well is a source of pride.
ZRRRPPPT

Since we focus on the finished work -- the ships -- it's easy to forget that the wood had a former life as trees.
SKREEEENK

Or that those trees are felled by people who appear to see their labor as a source of pride.
KREK

I'd met the merchants and sailors who delivered the timber, of course...
...but I'd never really thought about where the wood came from...

...until I found myself
observing an entire
SOCIETY of loggers.

A city of sorts, but a transient one.
How strange not to be bound to one island or province...but they appeared to be a thriving community.
And it reminded me so much of home. There was noise! Busy, not angry, sounds, and not the broken-spirit silence of Akasia.

Even so, it didn't seem wise to reveal myself right away.
But the loggers had ships, and I desperately needed one.
If I told them my story, would they believe me? Would they be willing to help?
People, I've learned, can act differently to outsiders than to their own.
So I decided to keep my secrets but to take a leap of faith...
...walk right up to them, ask for help...

...and find out what their reaction would be.
Aaah... HULLO?
EH?
WHO?
AKASIA?
GOTTA BE. THAT'S THEIR COLORS.
ANOTHER ONE?
ARE YOU ALL RIGHT?
OH, YOU POOR THING!
ARE YOU HURT?
DO YOU NEED ANYTHING? FOOD? WATER?
COME, WE'LL GET YOU SOMETHING TO EAT.
THANK YOU, BUT...
I was pleased that they seemed so caring...
...but the people of Akasia had also been caring.

...WHAT I COULD USE MOST IS A BLACKSMITH'S HELP WITH *THIS*.
SO YOU *DID* ESCAPE THE FACTORIES...
WE SEE ONE'A YOU EVERY NOW 'N' THEN.
HOW LONG DID YOU LAST?
YOU'RE NOT PALE ENOUGH TO BE A LONG-TIMER.
QUIT QUIZZIN' THE KID, HONDELL.
SHE'S CARRYING ENOUGH OF AN EXTRA LOAD...
...SHE DOESN'T NEED YOUR CURIOSITY PILED ON TOP.
COTSON HERE, THEY DUMPED HIM IN THE TOXIC SWAMP AS A YOUNGSTER.
ONLY HIS HEAD, THAT IS.
REALLY?
SURE!
GAVE ME THE BRAINS *HONDELL* DOESN'T HAVE.
BUT HE'S JUST PULLING YOUR CHAIN, MISS...?
SEPHIE.
SEPHIE, LET ME SHOW YOU WHERE YOU CAN HAVE THAT FINE JEWELRY REMOVED.

SETHUN, SEPHIE HERE NEEDS HER LEG CHOPPED OFF.
WHAT?
LEG IRONS. WASN'T I SPECIFIC ENOUGH?
STEP RIGHT UP!
I *WAS* HOPING TO *KEEP* THE LEG.
WE'LL SEE WHAT WE CAN DO.
SETHUN'S BLIND, YOU KNOW.
BLIND, BOWLEGGED, AND DRUNK.
IT'LL ONLY HURT A *LITTLE*.
THAT'S VERY REASSURING.
DON'T WORRY.
IF THESE GUYS HURT YOU DOING A SIMPLE JOB LIKE BREAKING THAT SHACKLE...
I'LL KILL 'EM.
AAAAAH... YOU DON'T *REALLY* MEAN THAT?

SURE I DO.
BLIND OR NOT, IF SETHUN'S AIM IS THAT BAD, DEATH'S THE ONLY THING FOR HIM.
KLANGK
KRAKKK
SAVED AGAIN, SETHUN!
YOU'LL HAVE TO FORGIVE OUR BAD JOKES, SEPHIE.
WE DON'T GET OUT MUCH, AND THE TREES HAVE HEARD ALL OUR BEST ONES ALREADY.
SO...HOW'D YOU MAKE IT ACROSS THE BLIGHTED AREA ALONE?
YOU'LL FIT IN HERE JUST FINE, SEPH!
ALTHOUGH HUMOR'S BEST IF YOU KEEP IT ***BELIEVABLE***.
OH, I JUST KICKED ONE CELANAUG IN THE FACE WITH ***THIS,*** SHOVED THE REST OUT OF MY WAY, AND FLEW ON OVER THE RIDGELINE!
FUNNY!

WHAT A WASTED VOYAGE!

BOSCAU, TAKE NOTE -- I AM NEVER AGAIN SETTING FOOT ON AKASIA.
HAVE ALL TRADE SHIPS REROUTED AND ALL CONTRACTS RESCINDED!
SIR...

TO THINK THAT THE MINISTER OF A SEWAGE-STEEPED *SURFACE* CITY THOUGHT SHE COULD FOOL THE MINISTER OF *CADADOR* INTO SUPPLYING HER PETTY TRANSPORTATIONAL NEEDS!
SIR?
THEY'LL BE BANKRUPT WITHIN THE MONTH.
WHAT *IS* IT, LOROSI?

VISITORS.
WHAT IS ONE TINY SURFACE CITY TO THE MINISTER OF MIGHTY CADADOR?
LET IT FALL FROM YOUR THOUGHTS...

...YOU HAVE NO NEED TO WASTE YOUR WRATH ON IT.
WELL, MUSE!
AFTER YOUR DISAPPEARANCE, I ASSUMED YOU'D ABANDONED ME.
I WAS *DISAPPOINTED*.
I HAVE MY OWN WAYS AND MY OWN PATH.
PUT ASIDE YOUR NEEDLESS ANGER, MINISTER OF CADADOR. I HAVE SOMEONE IT WOULD WELL SERVE YOU TO MEET.
MISS TERAMU AND I HAVE ALREADY BECOME ACQUAINTED.
NICE TO HAVE YOU HOME AGAIN, MINISTER.
HEED ME, FOOLISH MAN.
SHE IS NOT THE ONE.
THE *EYES* HAVE GAZED ON THE LINE OF YOUR FOLLOWING...YOUR FATE AND YOUR FUTURE.
YOU CONTROL MUCH OF THIS WORLD.
THE TIME HAS COME TO TAKE THE REST.
AS *THESE* INTRODUCTIONS ARE EXCHANGED, SO GROWS YOUR POWER.

GREETINGS, ILAHN, MINISTER OF CADADOR.
I HAVE COME AN EXCEEDINGLY LONG WAY TO MEET YOU.

RHO RHUSTANE, MINISTER ILAHN.
GREETINGS... ah, HAVE YOU A TITLE?
NOT HERE.
HERE, I'M JUST A MERCHANT.
THE LADY GIATAN, OUR MUTUAL ACQUAINTANCE, SPEAKS HIGHLY OF YOUR BUSINESS ACUMEN.
DOES SHE.
IT'S TRUE MY EFFORTS ON BEHALF OF CADADOR HAVE BEEN HIGHLY SUCCESSFUL.
SO MUCH SO THAT NEWS OF YOU HAS DRAWN ME ALL THE WAY FROM *ELYSIA*.
I WAS HOPING YOU COULD MAKE SOME TIME FREE FOR A FELLOW BUSINESSMAN TO DISCUSS A MUTUALLY BENEFICIAL PROPOSITION.
HMMMMM...I KNOW DEMETRIA WELL, BUT I'M NOT FAMILIAR WITH ANY CITY NAMED *ELYSIA*.
THAT IS BECAUSE ELYSIA IS ***NOT ON DEMETRIA,*** MINISTER OF CADADOR.
NOT ON--
HOW *INTERESTING*.
RHO, WAS IT?
LET'S DISPENSE WITH TITLES.
CALL ME ILAHN.
PLEASE-- HAVE A SEAT.
TELL ME OF YOUR FAR CITY...

SO...
AFTER LEAVING MY UNCLE'S CITY AND...FINDING MYSELF IN AKASIA, I WAS FIRST WELCOMED AS THE MINISTER OF MERIDIAN AND THEN CHAINED AS A POLITICAL PRISONER.
I MANAGED TO...PULL MY CHAINS LOOSE AND...WANDERED UNTIL I FOUND YOU HERE.

I HAVE TO GET HOME TO RAISE AN ARMY AGAINST ILAHN.
IF HE IS NOT STOPPED, *ALL* OF DEMETRIA WILL SOON BE UNDER HIS CONTROL.
ILAHN IS A MONSTER.

HE'LL DO ANYTHING TO ACHIEVE ABSOLUTE POWER.
I...MIGHT BE THE ONLY ONE WHO CAN STOP HIM, BUT I NEED YOUR HELP.
LEND ME A SHIP TO GET BACK TO MERIDIAN, AND I'LL SEND BACK TWO TO REPLACE IT.
AND JUST HOW DO WE KNOW THAT'LL HAPPEN?

YOU HAVE MY PROMISE AND MY WORD AS MINISTER OF MERIDIAN THAT NOT ONLY WILL YOUR SHIP BE REPLACED, BUT I'LL...
...*WE'LL* FIX AND STRENGTHEN YOUR ENTIRE FLEET.
WE MAKE OUR FORTUNE BY GETTING WHAT'S HERE OUT OF HERE BY THOSE SHIPS.
WE CAN'T JUST HAND ONE OVER ON EVEN THE BEST PROMISE.
BUT PART OF OUR LOAD'S DUE FOR MERIDIAN...
...IF YOU'LL JUST WAIT, WE'LL DELIVER YOU HOME.

SO WHO IS THAT GIRL, WILEM?
SHE WALKED OUT OF THE WOODS, HONDELL SAYS.

OH?
FOR A RUNAWAY, SHE SEEMS...SO *INTENT.*
DON'T GET DISTRACTED, GERRIS.
AFTER WE GUIDE THIS LOG UNDER THE BARGE, WE'LL GO JOIN THEM.
CUT YOUR LINE NOW.

GERRIS!
ROPE!

GOT IT...

GOT THE WRONG ONE--
THE STACK'S FREE!

WATCH IT!
KRAAAK
SNAP
SNAP
SNAP
I GOT IT!
NO!
DON'T TRY TO GRAB IT BACK!
GET AWAY!

OH, NO...
HEY-- UP! MOVE THE BARGE!

KRAK
I CAN'T BELIEVE THIS IS HAPPENING!
KRAAAK

KREAKK
YAAAAH
KRAK
WHUMP
HUNH!
KRAK

Accidents are a fact of life.
As disappointing and horrifying as they are...

...it's like we say, "we plan and prepare, but can't avoid fate's stare."

The bright side of those moments of crisis is that they also offer us the opportunity to find we can do far more than we ordinarily could

Which left me with a dilemma.
I could do e than an nary person.
Should I try to help?
Would my strange power hold back the rising timbers?
There was no one I could turn to for guidance...
...Papa's teachings never accounted for this.
But I had no trouble making a decision.
The people of Meridian would never hesitate to come to the aid of anyone in trouble...

...and I was still and forever a daughter of Meridian.

So there was never a question.

I should...

I would...

...and I COULD!

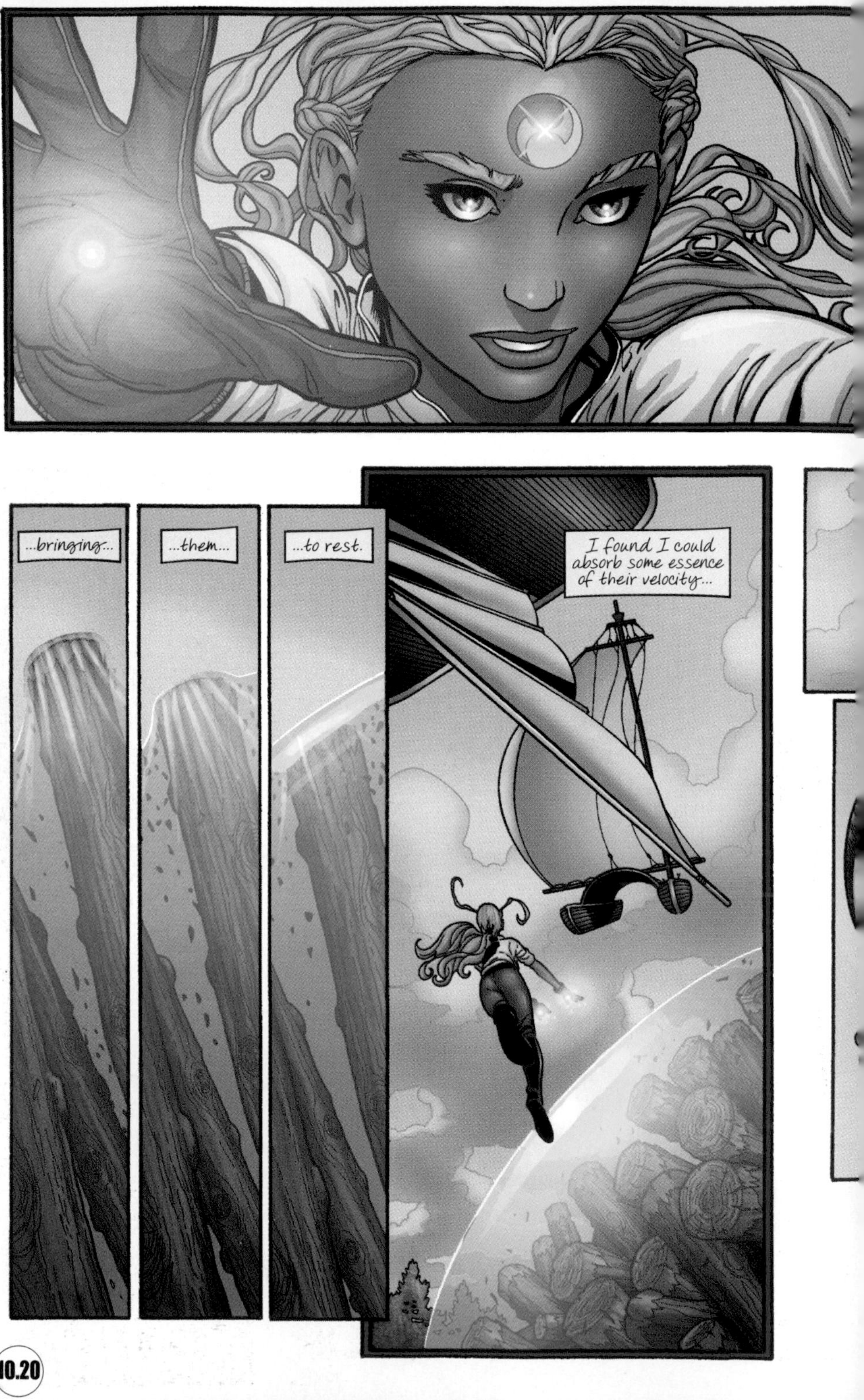

...bringing...
...them...
...to rest.
I found I could absorb some essence of their velocity...

Just as we sailors learn to feel and use the flow of wind around our ships to maneuver them through the sky...
...I was learning to play the effects of my own currents against the movement of the logs...

...making my task easier as it went on...

HUH. THAT GIRL'S FLYING, 'ROON.
I SEE THAT, BAERN.

...though it still wasn't EASY...

...but I did it!

Which left me only the question of what to do next.
They'd watched me.
They'd seen what I could do.
But how would they react?
I'd wondered what these people were truly like...
...now I'd find out.

MERIDIAN • CHAPTER ELEVEN

was taunting the Edge...
...but the monster who stole children from the rim of the floating-islands couldn't touch me.
The Edge would NEVER threaten me again...
I could FLY.
I was more frightened for Meridian than for myself.
I hoped my city was faring well under Uncle Ilahn's heavy-handed touch.
The stars shining overhead reminded me that Papa was watching over us both, Meridian above and me down below.
The loggers had shown me only kindness, even after my... display.
Even so, I'd needed some time alone to rest and just BE.
The surface world seemed so limitless, the way it rambled on and on...
...much like I'm doing now...
It was SO vast... during the day I'd seen the span of TWO Meridians...
...and no side of the other rim.
How strange, to live without knowing the limits of your world.

SEPHIE...
YES?
WHO'S CALLING ME?
KNOW ME.
IS ANYBODY THERE?
JUST ME, SEPHIE.
YOU REMEMBER ME, RIGHT?
Oh! SORRY, *GHETAN*.
FOR A MOMENT, I THOUGHT YOU WERE SOMEONE *VERY* DIFFERENT.

LOVELY PERCH YOU'VE DISCOVERED. WERE YOUR THOUGHTS AS DEEP AS THE CANYON?
I WAS JUST LOOKING AT THE STARS AND THINKING OF MERIDIAN.
I'M LOOKING SO FORWARD TO GETTING HOME.
YOU WILL GAIN YOUR ISLAND AGAIN, CHILD, BUT YOUR PATHWAY HOME TWISTS A TURN DEEPER BEFORE IT RISES TO THE CLOUDS...
WAITING FOR YOU DOWN BELOW IS A GIFT.
GO TO THE CAVERNS.
GO.

GO?
YES.
I THINK IT'S TIME TO REJOIN THE OTHERS.
YOU'RE RIGHT.
THEY'RE MY HOSTS. I'M BEING RUDE.

I'LL TELL THEM THEY DON'T NEED TO RUSH THEIR DELIVERY SCHEDULE ON MY ACCOUNT.
SINCE I'M ON THE SURFACE, I SHOULD KEEP ON TO THE ***CAVERNS***.
IF I GO HOME NOW, ALL I CAN DO IS MARSHALL MERIDIAN'S WEAKER FORCES AGAINST CADADOR'S TROOPS.
WE NEED ***ALLIES***.
There was something so comforting about Ghetan...
...so familiar...
...strange how I can't remember meeting him, yet it feels like I've known him forever.

NO ONE'S EVER TRIED TO GET THE CAVERNS AND THE SURFACE CITIES UNITED WITH THE SKY CITIES.

IF I CAN GET THEM TO JOIN ME, WE'D HAVE THE THREE PARTS OF TRADE--RESOURCES, CRAFTSMEN, AND TRANSPORTATION--WITHOUT CADADOR!

IF I CAN CONVINCE THEM IT WOULD WORK, WE CAN CREATE A COALITION WITH THE ECONOMIC POWER TO WITHSTAND ILAHN!

DO YOU THINK I'M DOING THE RIGHT THING?
IT'S A ***HARD*** ROAD YOU'RE PROPOSING, SEPHIE, BUT IT'S THE ONE MOST LIKELY TO CARRY YOU WHERE YOU NEED TO GO.
AS LONG AS IT LEADS TO MERIDIAN'S FREEDOM FROM MY UNCLE, IT'S THE RIGHT ROAD.

YOU READY, GERRIS?

DO YOU ACKNOWLEDGE YOUR MISTAKE?
YES... I DO.
BY NOT PAYING ATTENTION TO MY DUTIES, I PUT THE CAMP AND THE CREW AT RISK.
AND NOW YOU'RE READY TO FACE THE PRICE OF THAT LAPSE?
UHHHH, I--
SPEAK UP, BOY.
FILL THE WOODS WITH YOUR VOICE.
I'M GLAD NOBODY GOT HURT.
GLAD THAT THAT GIRL CAME ALONG IN TIME TO SAVE US ALL FROM MY DUMB MISTAKE.
I'VE MADE MY MISTAKE, AND NOW I'M READY TO TAKE MY PUNISHMENT.
CARRY THAT THOUGHT, BOY.
YOU'VE GOT A SHORT TRAIL AHEAD OF YOU--

"--BUT IT'LL BE THE LONGEST YOU'VE EVER WALKED."
CAN YOU FEEL THE WEIGHT OF YOUR MISTAKE, GERRIS?
SHAME ON YOU, LAD.
IT'S YOUR MISTAKE...
YOU COULD'VE COST US DEARLY...
YOU'LL NEVER FORGET NOW!
CARRY THAT BURDEN TO THE CHOPPING BLOCK.
YOU PUT THE WHOLE CAMP IN JEOPARDY, GERRIS.
YOU.
THAT'S A BIG MISTAKE.
ONE THAT WILL HAUNT YOU UNTIL IT'S PUT TO RIGHTS.

CARRY IT...
IT'S YOUR BURDEN
GERRIS
YOUR FAULT
GERRIS
A BIG MISTAKE
BEAR IT LIKE A MAN
CAN'T KEEP IT
FEEL THE WEIGHT OF IT
GERRIS
MISTAKE
CARRY YOUR MISTAKE
BEAR THE BURDEN
FOR THE GOOD OF THE CAMP AND THE ATONEMENT OF ALL--
--THIS ERROR MUST BE SACRIFICED AND *FED* TO THE *FIRE!*
STRIKE!
UNNN...
WHAT?!

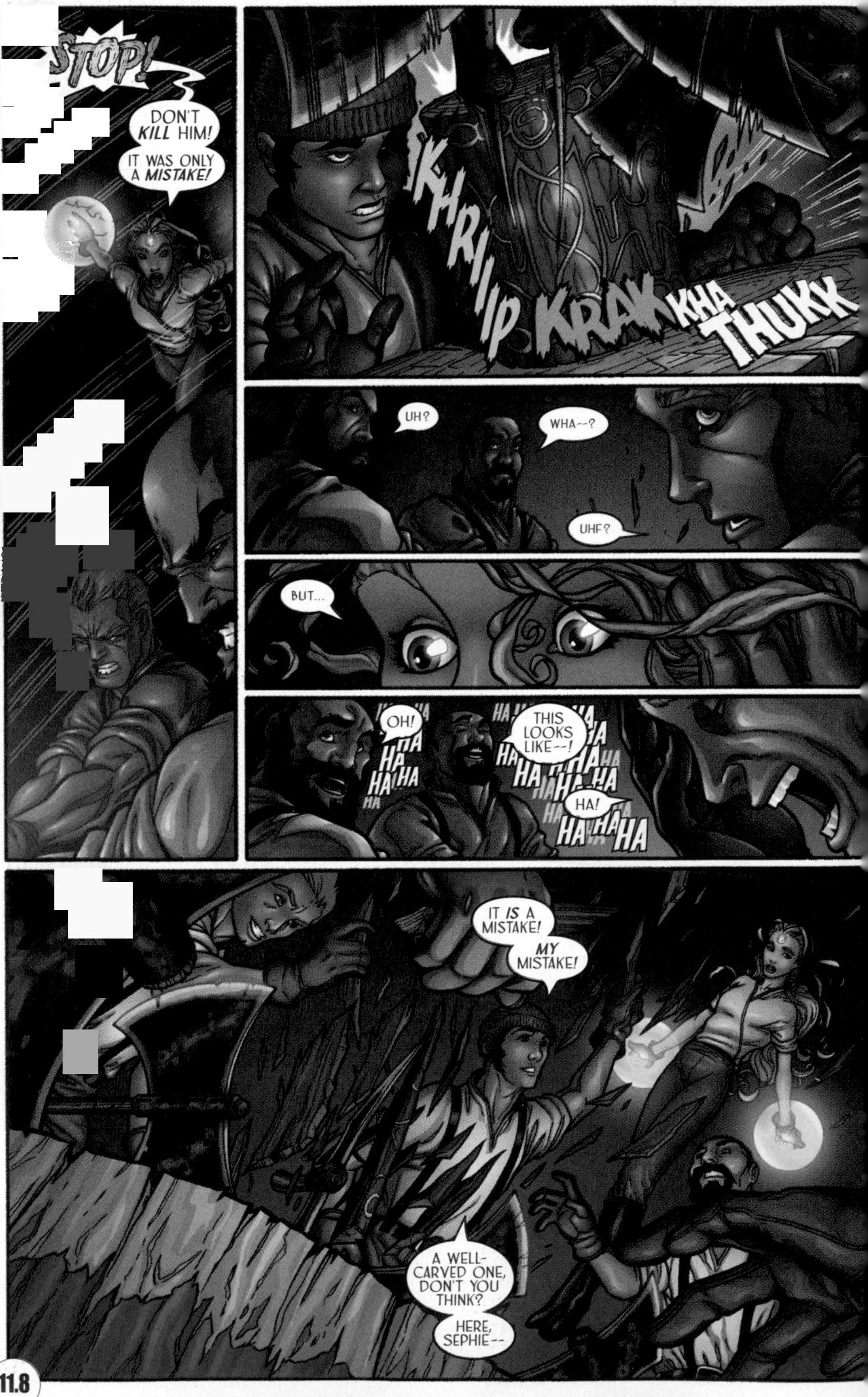

STOP!

DON'T *KILL* HIM!

IT WAS ONLY A *MISTAKE!*

KHRIIIP KRAK KHA THUKK

UH?

WHA--?

UHF?

BUT...

OH!

HA HA HA HA HA

THIS LOOKS LIKE--!

HA HA HA HA HA

HA!

HA HA HA

--FEED A SPLINTER TO THE FIRE AND HELP *ELIMINATE* IT!
WE ALL MAKE MISTAKES.
IF YOU DON'T FIND A WAY TO LET IT GO, YOU'RE STUCK CARRYING IT AROUND FOREVER.
SO WHEN WE SCREW UP, WE JUST CARRY IT A SHORT WAYS--
--BUT LONG ENOUGH TO REMEMBER THE HEAT OF ALL THOSE EYES ON YOU AND THE WEIGHT OF YOUR MISTAKE.

THEN YOU TOSS IT TO THE FLAMES AND MOVE ON.
I KNOW FROM EXPERIENCE THAT YOU DON'T MAKE THE SAME MISTAKE TWICE.
YOU CARVE *NEW* ONES.

MINISTER SEPHIE, *WE* DON'T WANT TO MAKE THE *MISTAKE* OF ALIENATING YOU OR MERIDIAN--

WE'LL MAKE A SHIP AVAILABLE TO YOU.
Oh!
THANK YOU, BUT...
YOU'RE DOING THE RIGHT THING.
...WHAT I REALLY NEED NOW ARE ALLIES.
AND INTRODUCTIONS.

I'M NOT GOING BACK TO MERIDIAN JUST YET...
...WHAT DO YOU KNOW ABOUT THE PEOPLE OF THE CAVERNS?

I KNOW THAT, SPARKLY HANDS OR NOT, IF YOU'RE GOING TO HEAD INTO THAT ROUGH WORLD, YOU NEED A *CREW.*
SOME OF US CAN BE SPARED FOR A TIME.
NO JOKE!
LET US *SHOW* YOU, NOT *TELL* YOU, HOW TO HANDLE YOURSELF IN THOSE PARTS.
DEAL?

I CAN'T EVEN BEGIN TO COMPREHEND WHAT SORT OF DEALINGS MIGHT BE GOING ON IN THERE!
THIS IS UNHEARD OF!
THEY'VE BEEN IN THERE ALL THIS TIME?
LOCKED IN, BOSCAU!
IT'S FILTHY IN THERE, I'M SURE, BUT HE WON'T EVEN ALLOW ME IN TO CLEAN!
HMPFH!
WHO KNOWS WHAT COULD BE SO IMPORTANT THAT HE'S SHUT US OUT?
I'M CURIOUS, RHO RUSTANE...
...WHAT REALLY BROUGHT YOU HERE TO CAPADOR FROM THIS CITY YOU COME FROM THAT IS NOT OF MY WORLD?
CERTAINLY IT'S NOT SIMPLY THE OPPORTUNITY TO DRINK WITH ME?
WHY CAN'T YOU BELIEVE I JUST WANT TO SHARE POWER WITH A LIKE-MINDED MAN?
hic
IS GENEROSITY UNKNOWN ON YOUR WORLD?

GENEROSITY ALWAYS HAS A PRICE--IF I ACCEPT POWER FROM YOU, I BECOME YOUR VASSAL.
I HAVE MY OWN POWER. THEREFORE, I DO NOT NEED YOURS. NOR DO I NEED A RELATIONSHIP OF DEPENDENCY.
YOU ARE THE STUBBORNEST MORTAL I HAVE EVER MET!
≥hic≤
I TAKE IT BACK.
I'M NOT SHARING WITH YOU.
HOW ABOUT SHARING IT WITH ME?
MISS TERAMU!
YOU--ARE NOT A PART OF THIS TRANSACTION!
I AM NOW.
WHAT DO YOU SAY, RHO?
WOULDN'T YOU PREFER AN APPRECIATIVE BENEFICIARY?
NOW THERE'S AN IDEA.
LAST OPPORTUNITY TO YOU, ILAHN.
≥hic≤
YOU TAKE IT, OR IT GOES TO HER.
AS I SAID BEFORE--
--QUITE CLEARLY--
-- I DECLINE YOUR OFFER.
SO I UNDERSTAND.
I HOPE YOU WILL NOT COME TO REGRET YOUR DECISION, MINISTER ILAHN.
MISS TERAMU!

>hic<
LET ME SHOW YOU WHAT IT MEANS TO BE TOUCHED BY THE POWER OF THE FIRST!
11.12

THERE'S OUR NEW HOME, LOUWEL.
ALL I SEE ARE A BUNCH OF ROCKS.

IT'S A NEW START IN TWO WAYS FOR US, MIRA.
IT'LL BE A TOUGH BATTLE, BUT SHE'S WORTH TAMING.
JON!
DO YOU MEAN THE NEW ISLAND OR ME?

I'M GLAD YOU LET ME COME WITH YOU, JAD, EVEN THOUGH I DON'T KNOW SHIPS.
STICK WITH ME, FEABIE, AND I'LL MAKE YOU FEEL YOU WERE BORN ON THE WIND!

JUREM--
--THE NEW ISLAND DOESN'T HAVE A NAME YET, DOES IT?
WHO GETS TO NAME IT?
THIS TRIP WAS JON TAKARTY'S IDEA, VIDRA.
SEEMS TO ME HE OUGHT TO HAVE THE HONOR.
KNOWING JON, THOUGH-- IT'LL BE PUT UP TO VOTE.

JAD?
DO WE--
I'M SORRY, FEABIE, I FORGOT YOU'RE NOT--
NO, I'M NOT, AM I?
I'M NOT *SEPHIE*.
I THINK I'LL MAKE YOU *PROVE* THAT TO ME.
TWO LONG, FEABIE.
KRANN

--DO WE
AVE TO GO
FIRST?
ABSOLUTELY!
ISN'T THIS INCREDIBLE?
WE'LL BE THE FIRST MERIDIANITES TO SET FOOT ON THE NEW MERIDIAN!
OH.
YES, THAT'S...
...WONDERFUL.
I'M JUST THE INEXPERIENCED ONE GOOD ONLY FOR RINGING OUT THE FLIGHT PATTERN TO THE OTHER SHIPS.
DON'T BE SAD, FEABIE.
YOU'RE SO MUCH MORE VALUABLE THAN THAT.
I'LL GET YOU THERE OKAY AND TAKE CARE OF YOU FOR A LONG TIME AFTER THAT.
WILL YOU?
KRANNNG

UP -- ONE SHORT.
KLANG
NOW TWO SHORT!
KLANG
KLANG
GET READY, FEAB!
ARE WE IN TROUBLE?
NAH --
THIS IS THE *FUN* PART!
ONE LONG!
KRANNNG
ONE LONG MEANS TO MY RIGHT?
IT'S *LONG* FOR THE HORIZONTAL PLANE AND SHORT FOR THE *VERTICAL* AXIS.
TWO LONG...
KRANNNG
KRANNNG
...ONE SHORT...
KLANG
...ONE SHORT AGAIN!
KLANG
ONE LONG...
IS THAT *AHEAD* OR *UP?*
BOTH -- IT'S USUALLY CLEAR WHAT'S NEEDED.
FEABIE, *HOW* DID YOU GROW UP WITHOUT EVER LEARNING SHIP'S CALLS?
KRANNNG

IT WAS SEPHIE'S JOB TO KNOW EVERYTHING ABOUT MERIDIAN AND ITS SHIPS.
IT WAS MY JOB TO TAKE CARE OF SEPHIE.
I'M SORRY SHE'S GONE...
...BUT I CAN'T BE HER FOR YOU, JAD.
HEY, LOOK AT ME...

...I'M JON TAKARTY'S SON.
THE FAMOUS CAPTAIN, ADVENTURER, COUNCILOR TO MERIDIAN...
...TUROS' BEST FRIEND, ET CETERA.
EVERYBODY LOOKS UP TO HIM.
THEN THEY LOOK AT ME AND WONDER WHAT HAPPENED.

I KNOW WHAT IT'S LIKE TO BE SECOND-BEST, FEAB, BUT YOU'RE YOUR OWN BEST SELF AND THAT'S ALL YOU CAN --
ONE SHORT! ONE LONG!
NOW!
NNGH!
AIEEEEE!
KRAAK
FEABIE!
KLANG
KRANNNG

NOT YOU, TOO...
NOT YOU.
GUESS THIS JUSTIFIES THE "ANNOYING SAFETY LINE?"
OW.
RELAX, FEABS. YOU JUST GET YOUR BREATH BACK AND I'LL HAUL YOU UP.
JAD...
...WILL YOU HATE ME IF I WANT TO STAY ON LAND FROM NOW ON?
I'D BE DISAPPOINTED--
--WHO'D RING MY BELL FOR ME?--
--BUT I'D NEVER HATE YOU.

KLANG
KRANNNG
KRANNNG
KLANG
KRANNNG
KRANNNG
KLANG
KRANNNG
KRANNNG

JAD'S THROUGH THE CATARACT!
YOU CAN SEE THROUGH THIS MURK? I ENVY YOU YOUR YOUNG EYES!

JON! GET OUT OF YOUR MAPS!
YOU'RE *MISSING* IT! THERE'S OUR NEW MERIDIAN!

NOW, MIRA, IT WON'T BE JUST LIKE MERIDIAN. WE CAN'T LET OURSELVES EXPECT TO HAVE IT BE AS--
OH, LOOK AT IT, JON!

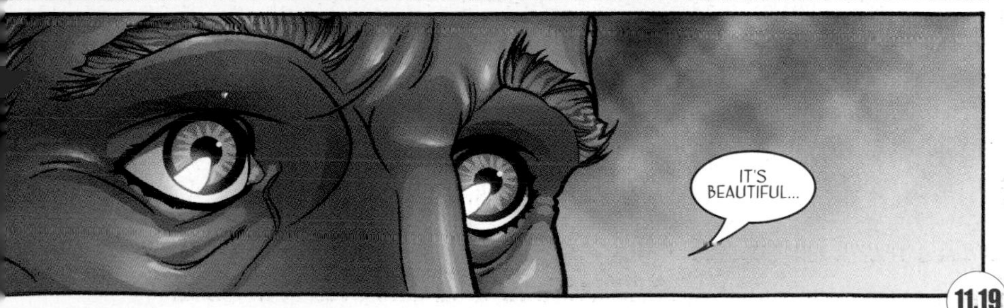
IT'S BEAUTIFUL...

"...JUST
BEAUTIFUL."

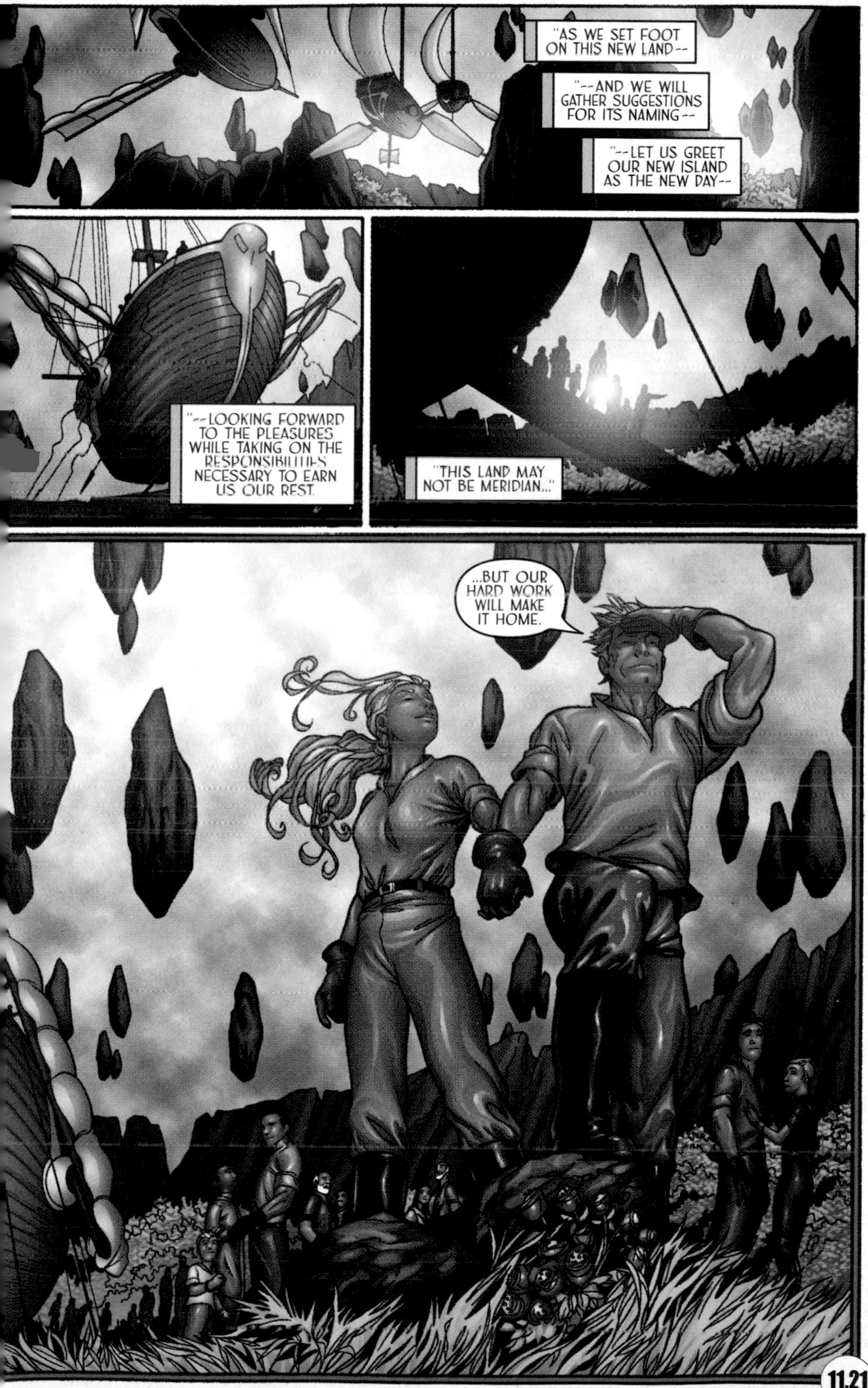

...BUT OUR HARD WORK WILL MAKE IT HOME.

Out of courtesy to my logger companions, I walked every step WITH them, not above them.
There'd be time enough to fly.
My next challenge was to be a good enough ambassador to the people of the caverns to win them to my cause.
It struck me then...
No sky city Ministers ever went to ground.
Representatives came up, but only trade ships went down.
It was time to forge a stronger bond between earth and sky...
...and I would be the link.

MERIDIAN • CHAPTER TWELVE

WHO IS THIS MAN YOU HAVE BROUGHT TO ME, MUSE?
WHERE DOES HIS POWER COME FROM? HOW COULD HE SO CASUALLY GIVE SOME TO REESHA?
DOES HE BEAR THE SAME SIGIL AS I, BUT CONCEALED?
SOMETHING SIMILAR, BUT NOT COMPLETE.
HE IS HERE TO BE BOTH SPUR AND LURE.
I SHOULD KNOW BY NOW THAT ALL YOU WILL OFFER ME BETWEEN YOUR DISAPPEARANCES IS A VAGUE SENSE OF MYSTERY, NOT *FACTS*.
YOU SEEM INTENT ON FORCING SOME *DIRECTION* ON ME...
...IS THIS RHO RHUSTANE PART OF YOUR VISIONS?
I SEE, AS ALWAYS, BEYOND THE NOW TO THE *RESULT*.
SOMETIMES I MUST COAX IT CLOSER.

STILL, YOU SHOULD HAVE CONSULTED ME BEFORE BRINGING HIM HERE.
INCLUDE ME, AND I WILL BE PARTY TO YOUR PLANS.
CONFOUND ME, AND YOU MIGHT FIND THAT I MAKE *YOU* AN AGENT OF *MINE*.
YOURS IS A FASCINATING SPIRIT, MINISTER OF CADADOR...
...UNFETTERED BY ANY CARE FOR OTHERS.
MY ONLY NIECE REJECTED ME, MUSE, AS DID HER MOTHER.
MY LINE ENDS WITH ME.
IT IS ONLY THROUGH MY *ACTIONS* THAT I WILL BE REMEMBERED...
...SO I WILL BE THE FIRST MINISTER OF *ALL* ISLANDS.
MY NAME WILL BE KNOWN FOR ALL TIME.

REESHA!
STOP THAT AT ONCE!
YOU'RE FRIGHTENING THE POPULACE.
IF YOU WISH, MINISTER ILAHN...
I TELL YOU, MUSE, THIS SITUATION HOLDS WITHIN IT THE SEEDS OF --
MUSE?
SIGH

...BUT I'M MERELY PRACTICING MY NEW SKILLS.
SURELY YOU WANT ME TO MAKE MYSELF...*USEFUL* TO YOU?
I'M SO DISAPPOINTED, MINISTER ILAHN.
I THOUGHT YOU'D BE PLEASED AT THE PROSPECT OF A TRUE PARTNER.
I HAVE NO PEERS, MISS TERAMU--
--JUST LESSERS OF MANY LEVELS.
ONE LAST GIFT, MY DEAR--
--A TALISMAN BY WHICH YOU CAN CONTACT ME, TO REMIND YOU TO *WHOM* YOU ARE BEHOLDEN FOR YOUR POWER.
AS A GUEST IS BEHOLDEN TO HIS HOST?
AS YOU ARE TO ME?
WILL THAT COURTESY BE REPAID WITH AN INVITATION TO VISIT YOU IN THIS... ELYSIA...FROM WHICH YOU HAIL?
AHHH...
PERHAPS...

"...BUT MY HOME MAY NOT BE AS INVITING AS YOU IMAGINE."
THE WATER SLAMS AGAINST THE DECKS *ALL DAY?*
ONLY IF YOU WATCH.
CLOSE YOUR EYES, AND IT ALL STOPS BUT THE ROARING.
SEPHIE, HOW COULD A GIRL FROM MERIDIAN NOT HAVE NOTICED THE OCEAN BELOW HER ISLAND?
I'VE SEEN IT FROM ABOVE, COTSON, JUST NEVER FROM THE *RIM!*
YOU WON'T WIN ALLIES AGAINST ILAHN IF YOU WASTE THE DAY STARING OUT TO SEA, SEPHIE...
AND WE'LL GET NO DRINK FOR OUR PARCHED TONGUES.
LET'S MOVE ALONG!
SEPHIE?
COMING, HONDELL.
TODAY?
PULL YOURSELF AWAY, GIRL...
...THE SEA'S NOT GOING ANYWHERE.

DO YOU KNOW WHAT IT'S LIKE INSIDE THE CAVERNS, SEPHIE?
I'VE HEARD STORIES, BUT ALL I'VE EVER SEEN OF THE SURFACE WORLD IS WHAT I'VE BEEN THROUGH ON THIS JOURNEY.

I KNOW A GAL. SHE KNOWS EVERYBODY AND EVERYTHING ABOUT THE CAVERNS, SO SHE CAN INTRODUCE YOU TO THE IMPORTANT PEOPLE, BUT SEPH --
--YOU'RE GONNA HAVE TO *SHOW* THEM HERE WHAT YOU CAN DO, AND SOON.
I DON'T KNOW ABOUT *THAT*...

LOOK AROUND--
THIS PLACE IS ON THE ROUGH SIDE, BUILT FOR GUYS LIKE ME.
MINING'S DANGEROUS WORK AND *THEY* DON'T WELCOME STRANGERS WHO'VE LED EASY LIVES UP IN THE SKY--*MUSCLE'S* VALUED HERE.

THEY WON'T *JOIN* YOU UNLESS THEY *RESPECT* YOU.
THEY WON'T RESPECT YOU UNLESS THEY CAN *FEAR* YOU A LITTLE.
ME, I'VE GOT HONDELL AND DANEYN HERE TO KEEP 'EM IN LINE.
YOU, YOU NEED TO SHOW 'EM YOU CAN KNOCK 'EM DOWN.
BUT BEFORE YOU CAN DO THAT...
KRAAK
WHUMP
THUDD
KERRAKK

...YOU'RE GONNA HAVE TO GET THEIR ATTENTION.

DEREN BEQ RUNS THE BEST MEETING HOUSE IN THE CAVERNS.
IN FACT, THIS PARTY PROBABLY STARTED AT HER PLACE.

SHE'S QUITE A WOMAN --THERE'S NOT A SOUL NEARBY WHO HASN'T FELT THE SOLE OF HER BOOT ON HIS BACKSIDE.
I'M NOT TALKING FROM PERSONAL EXPERIENCE, OF COURSE.
OW.

WAIT--LET ME TRY--
HEY, NOW--
DIDN'T KNOW YOU COULD DO *THAT,* SEPHIE.
NEITHER DID I. IT JUST SEEMED...POSSIBLE.
COTSON, YOU OVERSIZED PINHEAD!

DEREN BEQ.
PLEASED O MEET YOU, SEPHIE.
VATCH YOUR BACK--
--IT'S DANGEROUS HERE.
Oh, SHE'S JUST EXAGGERATING, SEPHIE. IT'S NOT ALWAYS LIKE THIS...
...SOMETIMES IT'S WORSE.
IT'S ALWAYS LIKE THIS. SWAT HIM IF HE TELLS YOU OTHERWISE.
NOT TOO MANY PEOPLE END UP DEAD, THOUGH.
STICK WITH ME.
I'LL KEEP YOU SAFE.
YOU'LL KEEP ME SAFE?

KRAAAAK
GRAAAH!
HEY!
FROM THIS?
SEPHIE, GET DOWN!
YOU'RE SAFE NOW.
I WAS ALREADY SAFE...
...AND SO WERE THEY.
I REALLY CAN TAKE CARE OF MYSELF.

HOW DID YOU DO THAT?
IT'S A VERY LONG STORY THAT STARTS WITH THE MARK ON MY HEAD...IT'S...IT'S PART OF WHY I'M HERE...
DEREN, SHE'S HERE TO GET OUT THE WORD ABOUT WHAT CADADOR'S MINISTER IS REALLY UP TO...
...AND GET PEOPLE LINED UP AGAINST HIM. SHE'LL NEVER HAVE A BETTER OPPORTUNITY TO GET EVERYBODY'S ATTENTION.
THIS FIGHT IS GETTING OUT OF HAND...
...IF I HADN'T CAUGHT THOSE TWO, THEY'D BE INJURED OR WORSE...
SO TAKE CONTROL! GRAB THIS GANG BY THE--
UH...
JUST SHOW 'EM, SEPH.
HMMM...
In a cavern full of brawling men and women...
...a situation that would have horrified me just DAYS ago...
...that was THE moment.
Something changed in me. If I was just SEPHIE when I wandered in there, asking for help...
HOLD THIS.
THAT'S MY GIRL.
COTSON...
WHO IS...
...WHAT IS SHE?

...now I was the MINISTER OF MERIDIAN and I was DEMANDING help.
Papa always felt he gained the authority of Minister before he inherited the title...
...I already had the title, but I only just then found the authority.
STOP IT!

DEREN BEQ, I'D LIKE YOU TO MEET SEPHIE, MINISTER OF MERIDIAN.
I'D HEARD THE GIRL HAD--
WHAT'S THE MINISTER OF A SKY CITY DOING DOWN HERE IN THE CAVERNS...?
I'D CALL IT FLYING, MYSELF. BUT CALL IT WHAT YOU LIKE, IT'S HER LEARNING TO SHOW OFF.
LISTEN TO ME!
YOU'RE WASTING ALL THIS AGGRESSION FIGHTING EACH OTHER!
YOU WANT SOMEBODY TO FIGHT? I'LL GIVE YOU SOMETHING REAL TO FIGHT FOR!
WHAT WOULD BEING ABLE TO TRADE DIRECTLY WITH THE SKY CITIES WITHOUT MINISTER ILAHN'S CONTROL MEAN TO YOU?
BETTER WAGES? LESS DANGEROUS WORK?
HOW TOUGH ARE YOU?
SHOW ME!
ARE YOU TOUGH ENOUGH TO DEFY CADADOR AND SAVE YOUR FUTURE?
I KNOW HIS PLANS! IF WE DON'T UNITE AGAINST HIM SOON, ALL OF DEMETRIA, ALL OF US, WE'LL BE NOTHING BUT HIS SLAVES!
YOU SEE WHAT I CAN DO?
"HE CAN DO WORSE!"
YOU THINK THIS IS THE ONE?
SHE... COULD BE.
WE NEED TO TAKE HER DOWN.
I'LL ARRANGE IT.
MEET US BEHIND MY PLACE.

MERIDIAN.
I was Minister in exile, far from my home, but home was never far from my thoughts.
AND THEN JAD TOLD ME HE'D TAKE CARE OF ME FOR A *LONG* TIME.

BE CAREFUL, FEABIE.
YOU KNOW HOW HE FELT ABOUT SEPHIE, POOR NEW STAR THAT SHE IS NOW.
Even as I envisioned the island overrun with Cadadorian soldiers, her people forced to garrison strangers...
...I knew my friends would find a way to make something good come of it.

That's what we do on Meridian -- find the good in things.
It's always there.
YOU JUST MAKE SURE --
--AFTER OUR ESCAPE FROM MERIDIAN AND THE WHIRL OF BUILDING A NEW HOME HERE --
--YOU'RE NOT RUSHING INTO THINGS.

LIKE YOU AND ISAGO AREN'T?
ZOUKA, JAD SAID HE'S GOING TO TAKE CARE OF ME FOREVER AND I'M GOING TO MAKE HIM *PROVE* IT.
I JUST DON'T WANT YOU TO HAVE YOUR HEART BROKEN.
THAT WILL NEVER HAPPEN, ZOUKA!
JAD *LOVES* ME!
I AM SORRY THAT SEPHIE'S GONE, ZOUK...
...YOU KNOW THAT...
...BUT I'M NOT SORRY THAT HER LOSS LET JAD AND ME FIND OUR OWN HAPPINESS.
WE'VE LOST OUR HOME AND OUR SEPHIE, BUT YOU HAVE ISAGO AND I HAVE JAD AND WE STILL HAVE EACH OTHER!
SAY IT WITH ME...
SISTERS NOT OF BLOOD, BUT HEART, OURS A BOND NO FORCE CAN PART.
SEPHIE WOULD HAVE WANTED A HAPPY ENDING FOR ALL OF US!
I'M READY NOW.

WHAT WELCOME NEWS.
I WAS AFRAID YOU WERE GOING TO MAKE ME LATE FOR MY OWN WEDDING!
BUT IT'S OUR FIRST WEDDING, MIRA!

I WANTED TO LOOK PERFECT!
YOU LOOK WONDERFUL, MIRA!
JON'S SO LUCKY!
AS AM I.
THANK YOU, MARIBET!
FEABIE, ZOUKA--
NO MATTER *HOW* YOU TWO LOOK, YOU *ARE* PERFECT.

SHALL WE GET STARTED?
IT'S SO... *SMALL*.
IT'S NOT *RIGHT!*
REMEMBER HOW WEDDINGS WERE--
--AT HOME?
LET'S LOOK FORWARD, NOT BACK.
OUR MERIDIAN IS LOST NOW, GIRLS...

...LOOK AT THE MAGICAL PLACE WE'VE MADE OUT OF WHAT WE FOUND HERE.
A NEW START ON A NEW ISLAND...
...IT COULDN'T BE *MORE* RIGHT.

⇒SIGH⇐
YOU YOUNGSTERS TODAY.
ALWAYS SO EAGER TO RUN OFF AND GET MARRIED.
GOT ANY ADVICE FOR ME, OLD MAN?
HMMMM...
ALWAYS LISTEN TO YOUR SON AND DO EVERYTHING HIS WAY.
WHEN HE'S THE ONE POLISHING MY BOOTS?
NOT LIKELY.
THANKS, JAD.
SO--HOW'S THE OLD MAN LOOK?
WHATEVER MIRA SEES IN YOU, IT'S CERTAINLY THERE TODAY.
BUT YOU TWO COULD HAVE WAITED FOR US TO CONSTRUCT THE GREAT HALL, DAD.
NOW'S THE RIGHT TIME FOR THIS.
WE NEEDED A SHARED CELEBRATION DAY TO MAKE THE NEW ISLAND HOME.
AND DA-- JON-- YOU WANT TO BE A MARRIED MAN AGAIN!
BOTH, JAD.
AFTER ALL THE TRAGEDY WE'VE SHARED AND THE PAIN OF HAVING TO UPROOT AND LEAVE MERIDIAN...
...IT'S IMPORTANT TO HAVE THE COMFORT OF FAMILIAR RITUALS IN AN UNFAMILIAR PLACE...

"...AND I *REALLY* WANT TO MARRY MIRA!"
MIRA DRAJUNA...
...I ASK YOU HERE, IN THE LOVING PRESENCE OF OUR FAMILY AND FRIENDS, TO MAKE PUBLIC AND KNOWN OUR DECISION TO JOIN OUR HEARTS AND HANDS AS ONE.
JON TAKARTY...
...I JOIN YOU HERE, IN THE CIRCLE OF OUR NEIGHBORS, TO AFFIRM OUR DECISION TO LINK HEARTS AND HANDS...
...TO GIVE YOU MY PROMISE THAT I WILL STAY BY YOUR SIDE AS LONG AS THE SUN WILL SHINE.
AND I GIVE YOU MY OWN THAT I WILL BE BY YOUR SIDE UNTIL WE BOTH JOIN THE STARS IN THE SKY.

NOW, WITH A KISS, LET OUR LIVES BE SEALED TOGETHER.

LET THIS SAME KISS BE PROOF OF OUR PROMISE, WITNESS TO OUR BOND.

"FROM NOW ON, LET US BE KNOWN AS *ONE*."

Remembering Meridian... my friends...didn't leave me feeling as empty now as it had back on Cadador...
...or Akasia.
I could call to mind happy times without having to cry...

...or wonder if they ever thought of me.
It was good to know that I would never again be so lonely...

...now that I had so many new friends.

Cotson, Hondell, Daneyn... they all believed in me enough to leave their work and join me.

I thought Deren did too, so I welcomed her friendship...

WELCOME TO MY LAIR.

WATCH THE BROKEN GLASS.

IT'S VERY...

...VERY...

...*ROUGH*.

THIS PLACE SUITS THE CAVERNS AND MAKES ME A GOOD LIVING.

THAT'S ALL IT HAS TO DO.

YOU, NOW-- TAKING ON MINISTER ILAHN ALL BY YOURSELF?

THAT'S ROUGH.

BUT I BELIEVE YOU CAN DO IT, SEPHIE.

I'VE MET... OTHER PEOPLE WHO BELIEVE AS FIERCELY THAT THEY CAN CHANGE THE WORLD.

I'D LIKE TO BELIEVE YOU ALL *CAN*...

...BUT THE TIME I'VE PUT IN CLEANING UP AFTER DRUNKS AND BRAWLERS MAKES ME SUSPICIOUS...
...SEPHIE...
...THAT'S JUST... *AMAZING*.

HERE'S WHAT I WANTED TO SHOW YOU.
YOUR MOTHER DREW THIS, SEPHIE...
...IT'S ME.
YOU KNEW MY MOTHER?
I NEVER KNEW SHE CAME DOWN HERE...
MANY TIMES.
I REMEMBER HER AS A GOLDEN, BIG-BELLIED WOMAN WHO MADE BEAUTIFUL PICTURES APPEAR.
BUT SHE NEVER CAME BACK AFTER SHE HAD HER BABY...
...YOU.
I HATED YOU THEN FOR TAKING HER AWAY, ESPECIALLY AFTER WE LEARNED SHE DIED...
...BUT I DON'T HATE YOU NOW.
THANK YOU FOR CHANGING YOUR MIND!
YOU CHANGED IT. WHAT YOU SAID TO THOSE MEN OUT THERE...

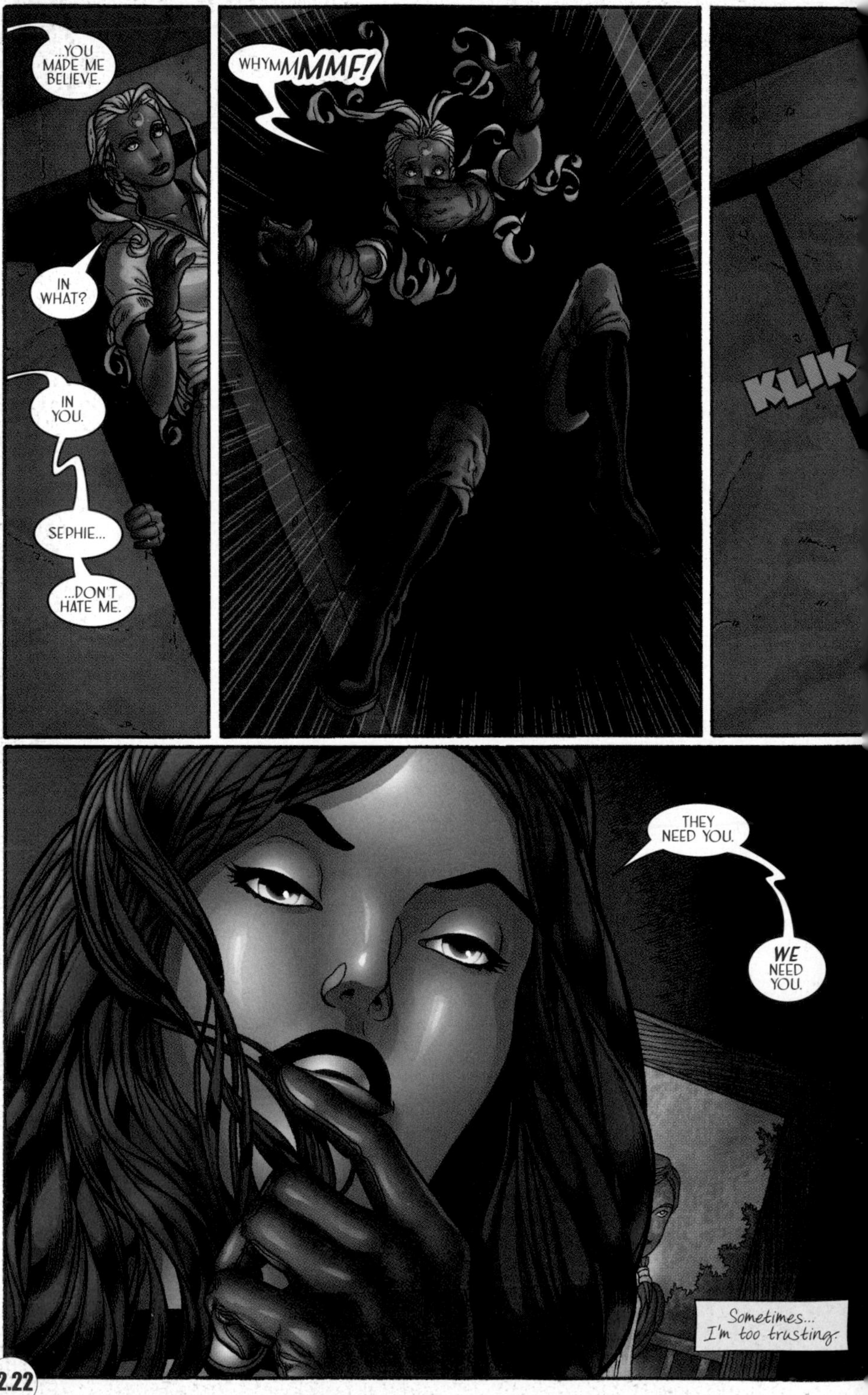

THEY NEED YOU.

WE NEED YOU.

Sometimes... I'm too trusting.

MERIDIAN • CHAPTER THIRTEEN

ood business is the equitable
xchange of goods and services.
When issues of power, manipulation, and control enter into the process, corruption takes root.
Just HAVING the advantage doesn't mean you should TAKE it.
Someone had tried to take ME hostage.
AGAIN!
They probably wanted to gain control of the power I'd just displayed... WITHOUT an exchange.
BAD business.
But THIS time I wouldn't end up in chains.
Not now that I knew what I could do.
WHO ARE YOU?!
DON'T YOU TOUCH ME AGAIN OR I'LL--

KILL US?
SEPHIE OF MERIDIAN, WE MEAN YOU NO HARM.
NOT MUCH CHANCE OF *THAT,* DREN.
IF SHE WERE THE KILLING KIND, WE'D BE ASHES BY NOW.
PLEASE DON'T.

MY APOLOGIES, MADAME MINISTER.
OUR SECRETIVE WAYS ARE LONG INGRAINED.
WE NEEDED PRIVACY TO APPROACH YOU AND THE LAIR'S PROPRIETRESS IS SYMPATHETIC TO OUR MISSION, AND SO--
HERE WE ARE.

DEREN KNEW YOU WERE--
SHE LET ME--
WHY?
WHO *ARE* YOU?

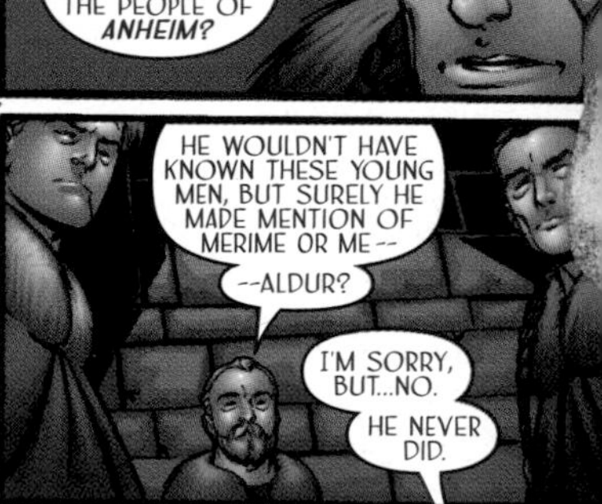
SEPHIE, DID YOUR FATHER NEVER MENTION THE PEOPLE OF *ANHEIM?*

HE WOULDN'T HAVE KNOWN THESE YOUNG MEN, BUT SURELY HE MADE MENTION OF MERIME OR ME--
--ALDUR?
I'M SORRY, BUT...NO.
HE NEVER DID.

THEN LET'S START OVER.
SEPHIE, WE ARE EMISSARIES OF THE SECRET CITY BELOW. WE'D LIKE TO TAKE YOU TO MEET WITH OUR MINISTER GERES.
YOU HAVE NOTHING TO FEAR FROM US--
--AND CLEARLY YOU COULD PROTECT YOURSELF IF YOU DID--
--BUT BOTH SIDES MAY HAVE SOMETHING TO GAIN.

GENTLEMEN, I'D BE HAPPY TO MEET WITH YOUR MINISTER...
...BUT NOT WITHOUT MY FRIENDS.
PLEASE GET THEM.

...BUT WHAT THEY ONCE HELD.
YES, AS FAR AS WE CAN DETERMINE, ANHEIM IS THE ONLY PRE-CATACLYSM CITY TO SURVIVE IN ANY FORM.
AS HER DESCENDANTS, WE ARE DEDICATED TO HER PROTECTION AND REVIVAL BECAUSE THE GARDENS PRESERVED HERE COULD BE THE KEY TO STOPPING THE DECAY OF ALL DEMETRIA!

ANHEIM'S SECRECY HAS BEEN CAREFULLY PROTECTED FOR *CENTURIES*.
WE RUN THE UPPER CAVERNS, SOME OF US--
VOLUNTEERS TAKE SHIFTS MANNING THE MAJOR BUSINESSES, GATHERING NEWS AND WHAT SUPPLIES WE CAN'T PRODUCE FOR OURSELVES.

WHILE THE OTHERS RUN THE ***DUNGEONS*** WHERE THEY HIDE THE ***GULLIBLE*** ONES WHO POKE AROUND INTO OTHER PEOPLE'S SECRETS AND END UP ***ROTTING*** AWAY IN--
WE HAVE NOTHING TO FEAR, COTSON.
I'D BE A LITTLE MORE COMFORTABLE HEARING YOU SAY THAT WHERE I COULD SEE THE STARS, SEPH.
THAT'S RIGHT... HOW DO YOU LIVE DOWN HERE WITHOUT LIGHT, CEREG?

THAT'S ONE OF ANHEIM'S SECRETS-- YOU'LL SEE WHEN WE ARRIVE.
YOUR VISIT IS A RARE EVENT-- VERY FEW PEOPLE ARE ALLOWED TO KNOW WHAT'S BELOW BECAUSE OF THE TREASURE PROTECTED THERE.
TREASURE?
NOT GOLD OR JEWELS...

OUR WEALTH IS NOT JUST WHAT THE CAVERNS HOLD NOW...

IT'S--
IT'S... ANCIENT!
Looking out over structures older than the original huts of Meridian wasn't half as surprising as what I suddenly noticed....
...the QUIET!
No wind, no crashing waves, no fighting-- the valley below was so STILL.
Yet, so ALIVE!

WELCOME TO ANHEIM, MINISTER OF MERIDIAN!

YOU MUST BE MINISTER GERES?

I AM, AND I NEED NO INTRODUCTION TO RECOGNIZE IDERIA'S CHILD!

I EXPECTED *YOUR* ARRIVAL-- WHO HAVE YOU BROUGHT WITH YOU?

PEOPLE OF THE LOGGING CAMPS WHO HAVE JOINED ME TO UNITE ANYONE I CAN CONVINCE AGAINST ILAHN OF CADADOR.

MAY I PRESENT MY FRIENDS HONDELL, DANEYN, AND COTSON.

UNIFICATION--ILAHN WASN'T QUITE THE THREAT THEN THAT HE IS NOW, BUT UNITY IS THE SAME GOAL YOUR PARENTS WERE HOPING TO ACHIEVE.
YOU KNEW THEM, *TOO?* AND PAPA NEVER SAID A THING!
HE RESPECTED OUR NEED FOR SECRECY, EVEN AS WE RESPECTED HIS NEED TO STAY HOME TO PROTECT HIS CHILD AFTER HIS WIFE'S M--
DEATH.

THEY MADE MANY VISITS HERE, SEPHIE.
WE VALUED THEM BOTH VE HIGHLY--

--AND I AM PLEASED TO SEE THEM BOTH IN YOU.
I WAS SORRY TO HEAR THAT TUROS HAD GONE TO JOIN YOUR MOTHER. HE AND IDERIA WERE BOTH INSTRUMENTAL TO THE IMPORTANT WORK WE DO HERE.
AS WILL BE THE DAUGHTER OF MERIDIAN.
WHA--?
WHAT ARE YOU DOING HERE?
THE EYES SEE ALL SECRETS.
WHAT YOU KNEW NOT, YOU NEEDED TO KNOW.
I SAW YOU HERE AND NOW YOU HAVE COME.
I WAS PLANNING TO DO THE HONORS, BUT I SEE THAT YOU AND THE MUSE OF GIATAN HAVE ALREADY MET.
NOT REALLY...
...SHE WAS...
...SHE WAS HELPING MY UNCLE ILAHN...
GUIDING, CHILD.
ONE SIDE CANNOT GROW WITHOUT THE OTHER.
AND THUS THE CIRCLE CONSUMES ITS TAIL, SO BEGINNING.
TAKE THIS, CHILD.

CAREFUL, SEPHIE--
IF SHE'S WITH ILAHN--
LET PAST MEET FUTURE, DAUGHTER KNOW MOTHER, THE SACRIFICE BE PAID.
IT'S ALL RIGHT, YOU TWO--
--I THINK I KNOW WHAT THIS IS...
IT'S *HERS,* ISN'T IT?
MY *MOTHER'S* ART.
IDERIA LEFT THESE HERE IN OUR SAFEKEEPING, KNOWING YOU WOULD COME...
NURSEBLOSSOMS...
THESE GREW OUTSIDE MY HOUSE IN MERIDIAN!

AND, THANKS TO IDERIA, THEY GROW HERE...
Ideria!
It was startling to think of her--
--of Papa--
--as travelers to distant lands.
Yet here was evidence that my mother--Ideria--was alive before she went to shine with the stars.
I know her only as a memory others have shared with me.

"...FOR SHE BROUGHT THE FIRST STALKS TO ME.
GERES!
WE'RE BACK!
"YOUR MOTHER HAD LOST HER PARENTS TO AN ACCIDENT LONG AGO.
"I'D LOST MY ONLY DAUGHTER IN THE BIRTH OF MY GRANDSON CRENNER, SO THE TIE OF TRAGEDY MADE NEW FAMILY OF US.
"THEIR JOURNE VARIED AS TH TRIED TO BUIL A BENEFICIAL COOPERATIVE A POLARIZED COLLECTION OF RIVAL CITY-STATES...
"NOT A SIMPLE TASK...
"...BUT IDERIA NEVER FAILED TO REMEMBER TO BRING A CONTRIBUTION TO YOUR COLLECTION AND MINE."
I'VE GOT TWO SURPRISES. THE FIRST IS THESE LOVELY FLOWERS. THE AROUDI CALL THEM NURSEBLOSSOMS.
THEY HAVE THE MOST WONDERFUL SCENT AND THEIR NECTAR IS USED FOR TREATING WOUNDS.
I'VE PLANTED SOME ON MERIDIAN, BUT I DON'T KNOW IF THEY'LL SURVIVE IN ITS COLDER CLIMATE.
WE'VE HAD A GREAT SUCCESS SINCE YOUR LAST JOURNEY. WE NOW HAVE A DROUGHT-RESISTANT VINE THAT THRIVES ON THE SURFACE TOXINS.
I'LL GIVE YOU SOME TO SHARE ON YOUR TRAVELS AND SEE IF THEY'RE AS SUCCESSFUL PLANTED ELSEWHERE.
SUCCESSFUL PLANTING?
WE'VE HAD OUR OWN, GERES.
AFTER SO MANY BARREN YEARS...
FINALLY...
...I'M CARRYING OUR DAUGHTER.

AYAHAAHAA!

HEAR THAT, CRENNER?

WHEN YOU GROW UP, YOU CAN MARRY MY LITTLE GIRL!

IT'S NOT BORN YET, TUROS. YOU MIGHT HAVE A SON!
TRUE.
MIGHT.

AND IF SHE'S HALF AS BEAUTIFUL AS HER MOTHER, YOU WILL BE SO LUCKY!
UHH?

SO, GERES, THIS WILL BE MY LAST TRIP TO ANHEIM UNTIL AFTER THE BABY IS BORN.
THAT'S UNDERSTANDABLE, AND COMPLETELY RIGHT.
YOUR DUTIES MUST TURN MORE PERSONAL THAN POLITICAL NOW.

I'LL MISS YOU, BUT IT'S TIME FOR YOU TWO TO REST AWHILE.
THANKS TO YOUR YEARS OF WORK, WE'VE MADE GREAT PROGRESS IN OUR GARDENS.
WE THINK WE'VE ACTUALLY BEGUN TO HALT THE DEGRADATION OF DEMETRIA.
BY YOUR DAUGHTER'S TIME, WE MAY HAVE BEGUN ITS HEALING.
WE MAY EVEN BE ABLE TO DO OUR WORK OPENLY.
I'D BE CAUTIOUS ABOUT THAT.
YOU KNOW TUROS' BROTHER IS MINISTER OF CADADOR NOW, WITH EUDORICE AND CLAIRESSA DEAD?
DO YOU KNOW HOW MUCH POWER HE'S GAINED, AND WHAT HE WOULD DO IF HE KNEW ANHEIM EXISTED?
HE'D WANT TO CONTROL, CONTRACT, AND TAX WHAT YOU'RE DOING HERE.
YOU DON'T TRUST ILAHN?
I HATE TO SPEAK ILL OF ANYONE, BUT DEATH SEEMS TO FAVOR HIS PLANS...
ILAHN WANTED ME, GERES, BUT IT WAS TUROS I LOVED.
THANK THE STARS ILAHN'S NEVER CONSIDERED TUROS AN IMPEDIMENT TO HIS POWER-HUNGRY SCHEMES.
I COULDN'T BEAR IT IF--
--IF--

ENOUGH TALK ABOUT THAT MONSTER!
CARE TO SEE MY LATEST CANVAS?
OF COURSE!
A SELF-PORTRAIT?
IT BEGAN AS ONE, BUT THOSE FLOWERS WERE SO LOVELY THAT I HAD TO PRESERVE THEIR BEAUTY.
YOUR GARDENS CAN DO THE SAME FOR THE LIVING, GERES.
BUT, IDERIA, IT WAS ONLY A VISION. THE TRUTH SOMETIMES DIFFERS...
WHICH IS WHY I'VE NEVER TOLD TUROS.
YOU AND THE MUSE ALONE SHARE MY SECRET KNOWLEDGE.
IF IT SHOULD COME TO PASS THAT I... GO...BEFORE MY TIME...
...HELP PROTECT THEM BOTH--THE NURSEBLOSSOMS...
...MY DAUGHTER--

"--LET SOME PART OF ME BE PART OF DEMETRIA'S HEALING."
I'VE ALWAYS LOVED NURSEBLOSSOMS, BUT I'VE NEVER SEEN ANY SO...
13.14

RASE!
WHO'S THAT-?
...HEALTHY.
CRENNER, TOO MUCH TIME SNIFFING THE FLOWERS AND NOT ENOUGH PAYING ATTENTION TO THE NEWS!
THAT'S HER!
TUROS AND IDERIA'S DAUGHTER.
THE FLYING ONE FROM MERIDIAN?
THAT'S THE MINISTER OF MERIDIAN?
IT IS HEALTHIER.
WE'VE WORKED TIRELESSLY TO ENHANCE THE PLANT'S HEALING PROPERTIES.
WE EXPORT THE NECTAR THROUGH AN AGENT IN BASAN. YOU MAY KNOW THE FINAL PRODUCT ALREADY...
BASANTY SALVE? THAT'S REALLY JUST NURSEBLOSSOM NECTAR?
BASIC BUSINESS, MINISTER SEPHIE.
I KNOW, I KNOW-- IT'S ALL IN THE SHOWING.
PRESENT YOUR LOCAL GIFTS AS GOLD.

THEN MAY I ADD TO YOUR WEALTH WITH THIS LOCAL BEAUTY!
THANK YOU.
IT'S A WONDERFUL GIFT!
THESE FLOWERS ARE MY PARENTS' LEGACY AND NOW I HAVE ONE IN ART AND IN LIFE.
DO YOU TEND THEM?
HE NOT ONLY TENDS THEM, HE'S FAST BECOMING OUR GARDENS' MASTER BOTANIST.
SEPHIE, HERE IS MY LEGACY--I'D LIKE YOU TO MEET MY GRANDSON CRENNER.
LATELY, HE'S BEEN ROOTING THROUGH OLD SEEDS STORED IN THE RUINS AND HAS MANAGED TO BRING BACK SOME LOST STRAINS.
ANHEIM'S HISTORY WILL LIVE AGAIN THROUGH HIS WORK, SEPHIE...
...JUST AS MERIDIAN LIVES ON THROUGH YOU.

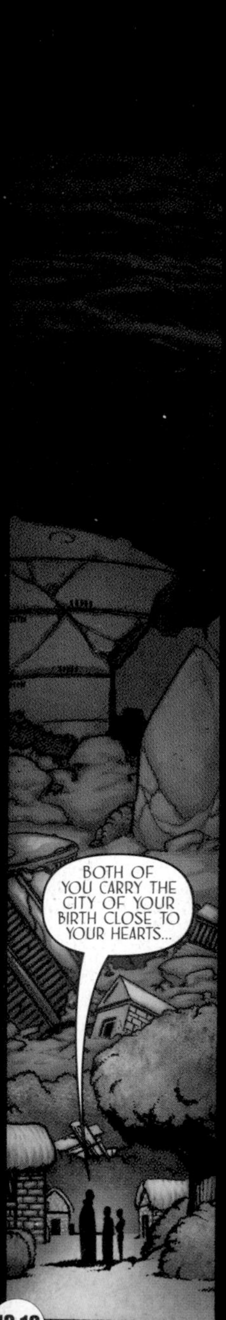
BOTH OF YOU CARRY THE CITY OF YOUR BIRTH CLOSE TO YOUR HEARTS...

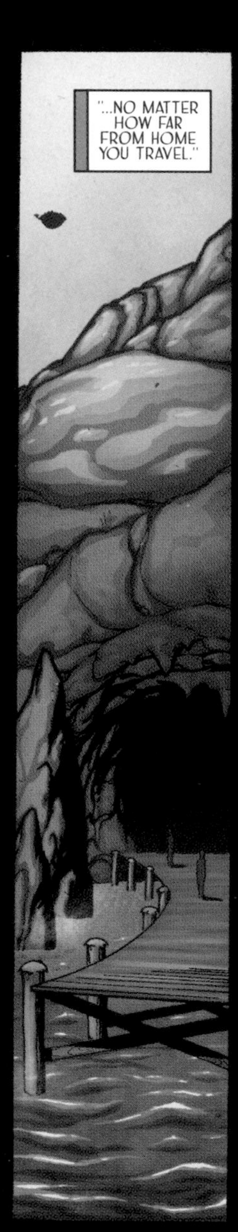
"...NO MATTER HOW FAR FROM HOME YOU TRAVEL."

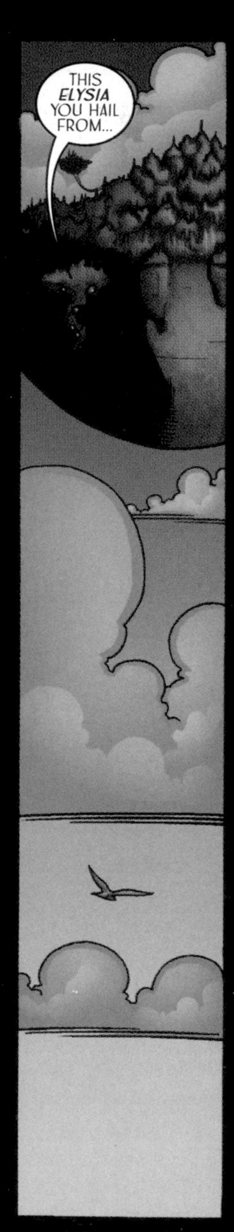
THIS *ELYSIA* YOU HAIL FROM...

...THIS RADIANT HOME THAT IS FAR FROM CADADOR...

...COULD ONE PLOT IT ON A MAP?
MINISTER ILAHN, LADY REESHA--
AS THE STARS ARE TO YOUR EYES, SO IS ELYSIA TO DEMETRIA. TOO FAR REMOVED FOR YOUR MAP.
THEN HOW DID YOU COME TO BE HERE?
YOU MUST HAVE SOME FORM OF TRAVEL--
--LIKE A BIRD!--
--THAT BRINGS YOU FROM THIS STAR-DISTANT HOME OF YOURS!
TAKE E THERE, RHO.
I WANT) SEE THIS TY YOU SAY WARFS MY OWN.
ILAHN, I CAN'T JUST SHOW UP ON THE GRAND PLAZA WITH STRANGERS!
INGRA WILL HAVE MY--
SO--YOU HAVE THOSE YOU ANSWER TO?
YOU ARE MERELY THEIR AGENT?
SCOOT, VILL YOU, OROSI?
CAN'T SEE.
EEEE!
I DON'T ANSWER TO--!
IT'S JUST THAT--!
IT'S NOT LIKE THAT AT ALL!
YET IT *IS*.
IF YOU CAN'T INVITE VISITORS TO YOUR HOME VITHOUT *THEIR* PERMISSION, THEN YOU ARE--
I AM OF THE FIRST!
I CAN DO WHATEVER I WISH!

THEN SHOW ME HOW YOU TRAVEL TO--
MINISTER ILAHN?
MINISTER ILAHN...
...YOU HAVEN'T JUST...
...DISAPPEARED

--ELYSIA.
VERY GOOD!
I KNEW I'D WEAR HIM DOWN.
NOW, IF YOU'LL DELIVER ME TO YOUR MASTERS, RHO RHUSTANE...
MINISTER ILAHN...
THAT MIGHT NOT BE HIS NAME IN THIS FORM.
HNNH?
OH.

WELCOME TO *ELYSIA,* MINISTER OF CADADOR.
THIS IS WHERE *WE* GO ABOUT OUR BUSINESS.
THIS CHAOS?
YOU OBVIOUSLY SOUGHT ME OUT FOR MY PROFESSIONAL ADVICE.
INTRODUCTIONS, RHO.
SHALL WE BEGIN?
Somewhere out there, I knew Uncle Ilahn was plotting against Meridian.
It was comforting to be in the presence of secret allies and know he didn't share that advantage.
Now all I needed was enough time...

I have no letters from my mother. She left no journal of her days. No messages to me.
Papa always said she expressed herself better in pictures than with words.
She died before I was old enough to remember her, so I don't know the look of her face or the sound of her voice...
...but these pictures capture her spirit in every line.
For the first time, I feel I know her.
Papa's told me of the day they met... again the feast day of a new ship's completion...
JON?
WHO IS THAT?
YOU REMEMBER THE GARSKENS, THE SHIP DESIGNERS?
THEY'RE JUST BACK FROM THEIR DESIGN TOUR OF DEMETRIA WITH WONDERFUL PLANS FOR A NEW ONE-MAN SHIP AND...
...THAT'S THEIR DAUGHTER.
IDERIA?
THE SKINNY ONE ALWAYS SPATTERED WITH PAINT?
THAT'S HER?
IT'S BEEN MORE THAN A FEW YEARS, 'ROS.
WE'RE DIFFERENT, TOO.
JON...

"...I THINK I REALLY OUGHT TO WELCOME HER HOME TO MERIDIAN *PERSONALLY!*"

IDERIA!
LEAVE YOUR CHALKS AND COME BACK TO *THIS* WORLD, DAYDREAMER--
--HERE'S ANOTHER OLD FRIEND TO MEET AGAIN.
HULLO, JON, AND WHO'S WITH YOU?
IDERIA--
--I DIDN'T EVEN RECOGNIZE YOU!
I SHOULD HAVE--AND IF I'D LOOKED AT YOUR ART *FIRST,* I *SURELY* WOULD HAVE...

Oh, NO.
WHAT IS IT?
TROUBLE, DEAR.
TAKE A LOOK.

OUR DAUGHTER, THE MINISTER'S SON--
--THAT'S A PATH TO CERTAIN DISAPPOINTMENT.
IT'S TUROS, IDERIA.
I HOPE YOU REMEMBER ME AFTER SO LONG.
ARE YOU HOME TO STAY, I HOPE?
Oh, NO.
JUST UNTIL THE NEW SHIP'S LAUNCHED.
THEN I'M OFF ON MY OWN SOLO JOURNEY, TUROS...?
THEY'RE JUST *TALKING,* DEAR.

TUROS...?
TUROS!
Oh.
YOU'RE THE MINISTER'S SON!
AAAH...
EXCUSE ME, PLEASE.
I--
I HAVE TO GO-- *OOOF!*
WHY, *IDERIA...*

...I WAS HOPING I'D RUN INTO YOU, ALTHOUGH NOT QUITE SO LITERALLY.
YOU RECOGNIZED ME?
THAT'S BEEN A RARE EVENT TODAY.
HOW COULD I NOT?
YOU HAVEN'T CHANGED A BIT--

--YOU'RE STILL AS BEAUTIFUL AS EVER.
I HEARD YOU'VE BEEN ADVENTURING, COLLECTING IMAGES FROM ALL OVER DEMETRIA...

FOR WHICH YOU'LL NEED *THIS*.
TUROS.
Oh!

Oh, WERE YOU TWO CONVERSING, ILAHN?
SORRY TO INTERRUPT!
I'M NOT SORRY YOU--
I MEAN I--
THANK YOU, TUROS.
YES.
THANK YOU, TUROS.

PERHAPS WE'LL SEE EACH OTHER AGAIN, IDERIA.
WHEN YOU'RE NOT IN SUCH A *HURRY*.
PERHAPS WE SHALL, TUROS.
IT'S SUCH A SMALL ISLAND.

I REALLY MUST GO, ILAHN.
OF COURSE!
YOU HAVE TO PREPARE FOR YOUR DEPARTURE.
IT SADDENS ME TO HAVE YOU HERE FOR SUCH A SHORT WHILE...

...I'D LOVE TO JOIN YOU ON A JOURNEY SOMETIME.
AFTER ALL, I'M NOT LIKE MY *BROTHER*.

THE SECOND SON IS NOT *TIED* TO MERIDIAN AS *TUROS* WILL BE WHEN HE BECOMES HER MINISTER.
THE WHOLE OF DEMETRIA CAN BE MINE, SHOULD I WISH...

...AND YOU DESERVE SOMEONE WHO WOULD GIVE YOU THE WORLD.
GOOD DAY, IDERIA.

Mother created quite a sensation. She was nearly three decades old and she'd spent more of her life away from Meridian than on it.
At an age when most girls were long married and watching their own children grow, Ideria had no thoughts of settling down...
...and Papa knew this to be so, even as he spent his days in her pursuit.
HOW COULD I NOT BE READY TO PLOT OUT THE FIRST SOLO TREK OF THE INFAMOUS AND EXOTIC BEAUTY, IDERIA GARSKEN?
Oh, JON, PLEASE.
I'VE HAD ENOUGH OF THAT!
YOU'D THINK I'D BEEN GONE FOR CENTURIES AND TRANSFORMED FROM TROLL TO HUMAN!
JON!
ARE YOU READY FOR ME?

THE GULF BETWEEN GIRL AND WOMAN CAN SEEM AS FAR REMOVED TO US MEN.
LET'S SEE THOSE MAPS!
DO YOU NEED TO DELIVER THE NEW SHIP TO KENNIT RIGHT AWAY?
WITH MOTHER AND FATHER STAYING TO OVERSEE CONSTRUCTION OF THE NEW WASP DESIGN, I'M FREE TO TAKE AS LONG AS I LIKE. THERE'S A SMALL ISLAND TO THE SOUTH OF KENNIT I'D LIKE TO SEE.
WE'LL TOW THE NEW SHIP WITHOUT CREW, SO IT DOESN'T MUCH MATTER HOW LONG IT FOLLOWS ALONG.
IT'S YOUR CALL--WE CAN TAKE AS MUCH TIME AS YOU WANT, SEE WHATEVER YOU PLEASE.

I COPIED THIS MAP FROM THE MASTER OF AN AROUDAN SHIP.

ALONG THE EASTERN COAST OF THE LAND BENEATH REENDRAU LIVES AN ANIMAL WITH THE MOST AMAZING PELT.
I SAW ONE! THE FUR SHINES LIKE COPPER IN THE SUN!
I'D LIKE TO SEE IT AGAIN, IN *LIFE*...
DO YOU WANT TO STOP AT THE CAVERNS ON THE WAY?

THAT'S AN IDEA-- I'VE NEVER BEEN *INSIDE*.
I'D ALSO LIKE TO SEE...
...SEE...
...I'M SORRY, JON.
I JUST CAN'T SEEM TO CONCENTRATE.
HMMM?

I'D BEEN LOOKING FORWARD TO DESIGNING MY OWN JOURNEY SINCE...
I THOUGHT I'D ENJOY IT MORE, BUT...
...BUT NOW...

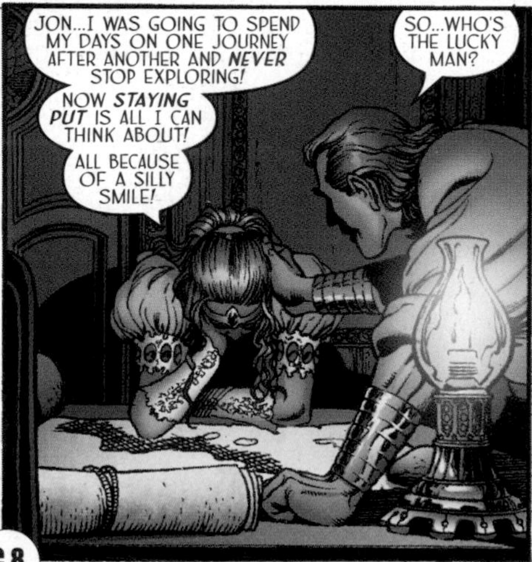
JON...I WAS GOING TO SPEND MY DAYS ON ONE JOURNEY AFTER ANOTHER AND *NEVER* STOP EXPLORING!
NOW *STAYING PUT* IS ALL I CAN THINK ABOUT!
ALL BECAUSE OF A SILLY SMILE!
SO...WHO'S THE LUCKY MAN?

NO ONE!
AND *DON'T* YOU TELL HIM!

"HE'S EVERYWHERE I GO, JON...
"AT FIRST HE JUST *HAPPENED* TO CROSS MY PATH...
"...BUT I REALIZED I'VE ALWAYS MADE SURE MY LOCATION WAS EASY TO SPOT!
"NOW IT'S GOTTEN TO THE POINT WHERE HE'S ALWAYS WITH ME..."
...EVEN WHEN I'M ALL ALONE.
I CAN'T LEAVE, JON...

...AND I CAN'T BEAR THE THOUGHT OF NOT EVER LEAVING AGAIN.
WHAT DO I DO?
THERE'S NO NEED TO RUSH A DECISION.
TEST BOTH DIRECTIONS AND SEE WHICH ONE PULLS STRONGEST AT YOUR HEART.
But a Durakan trade ship with a careless sailor and a full hold of ore made mother's decision for her.
They still tell the tale of that day.
Meridian, which needs no ore pods to stay buoyant, sees few such accidents.
But we are a practical people, so help was quickly organized.
But for mother...
NOOOO!
IDERIA!
STAY BACK! YOU CAN'T HELP THEM NOW!

.nothing could alve her wound.
.I know her agony... I've carried this same scream inside me since Papa died.
They were having a quick meal in the rim cafe when it happened...
Mother would have been with them...
...if not for Papa.
He assumed their union was only a matter of course...

...but mother had different thoughts.
SO YOU HAVE TO STAY ON MERIDIAN AND OVERSEE THE NEW SHIP FOR YOUR PARENTS.
IS STAYING HERE...WITH ME...REALLY SO BAD?
THERE ARE OTHERS WHO CAN SEE TO THE SHIP'S SUPERVISION-- LEAVE IT TO THEM.
COME AWAY WITH ME. LEAVE MERIDIAN AND YOUR PAIN BEHIND.
I WILL TREAT YOU LIKE A QUEEN.
IN FACT, ANY OTHER WOMAN WILL SUFFER BY COMPARISON.
IDERIA, CAN YOUR CONSCIENCE ALLOW THAT?
I'LL NEVER FORGET YOU. I'LL NEVER LET YOU GO.
DO YOU UNDERSTAND THE INTENSITY OF MY DEVOTION?
I SYMPATHIZE WITH YOUR LOSS, BUT I BRING SOME COMFORT--
I'VE CALLED IN NESCOAN'S TOP CARRIAGEMAKER TO OVERSEE THE SHIP'S CONSTRUCTION.
FREEING YOU TO LEAVE MERIDIAN.
WE BOTH KNOW THE WEIGHT OF RESPONSIBILITY.
I KNOW YOU AND MY SON...CARE FOR... EACH OTHER.
BUT HE HAS A RESPONSIBILITY TO MERIDIAN.
HE MUST MARRY A WOMAN...
...YOUNG ENOUGH...
...TO ENSURE AN HEIR.

Dearest Turos, I cannot stay on Meridian, even for you

Please remember me fondly when you see this

and always remember my love for you

Yours even in parting,
Iderea
For some unknown reason...

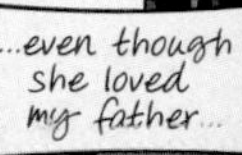
...even though she loved my father...

...mother decided to leave Meridian.

SHE WAS SENDING THIS TO...HIM, MASTER ILAHN.
WELL DONE, GHUTER...

...WELL DONE.

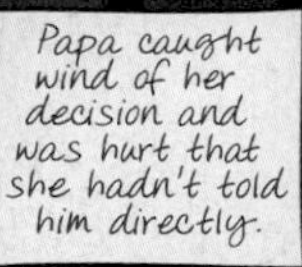
Papa caught wind of her decision and was hurt that she hadn't told him directly.

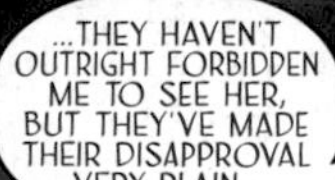
That, coupled with his family's advice to him to accept her departure, made him seek out Jon for his counsel...
...THEY HAVEN'T OUTRIGHT FORBIDDEN ME TO SEE HER, BUT THEY'VE MADE THEIR DISAPPROVAL VERY PLAIN...
I'M TO BE MINISTER SOMEDAY.
IDERIA IS GOOD FOR ME, BUT SHE MAY NOT BE GOOD FOR MERIDIAN.
MAYBE THEY'RE RIGHT.

TUROS...
...YOU SHOULD COME ALONG WHEN WE DELIVER THE NEW SHIP.
IT WOULD DO YOU GOOD TO GET AWAY FROM MERIDIAN FOR A WHILE.
NO...I... CAN'T.

YOU SHOULD.
YOU'VE NEVER BEEN MUCH OF AN ADVENTURER, TUROS.
YOU SHOULD GET OUT AND SEE A LITTLE MORE OF DEMETRIA BEFORE YOU RULE THE HEART OF IT.

RUNNING AWAY ISN'T GOING TO HELP ME, JON.
TAKING A LEAVE FROM YOUR RESPONSIBILITIES MIGHT.
KEEP IN MIND, THOUGH, THAT I'M THE CAPTAIN. ONCE WE'RE OUT ON THE WIND, I'LL BE THE SOLE AUTHORITY ON BOARD, NOT YOU.

EVEN THAT LOCAL ARTIST WHO'S CHOSEN MOST OF THE COURSE OF THE TRIP, SHE WILL HAVE TO RESPECT MY AUTHORITY.
I'LL BE THE ONE TO GIVE ORDERS, ENFORCE LAW, PERFORM MARRIAGES...
WHEN DO WE LEAVE?

"I'LL HAVE THE SHIPS READY TO PUSH OFF IN THE MORNING."

WILL YOU STOP FRETTING?

HE'S NOT *HERE,* JON...

...I THOUGHT HE'D BE HERE.

MINISTER DRACHE PROBABLY ADVISED AGAINST HIS PRESENCE HERE TODAY.

HE WAS NO DOUBT CONCERNED THAT TUROS MIGHT BE TEMPTED TO COME ALONG.

BUT TUROS WOULD *NEVER* LEAVE MERIDIAN.

NOT EVEN FOR ME.

YOU NEVER KNOW...

"...A MAN FINDS HIMSELF DOING MANY SURPRISING THINGS FOR THE RIGHT WOMAN."

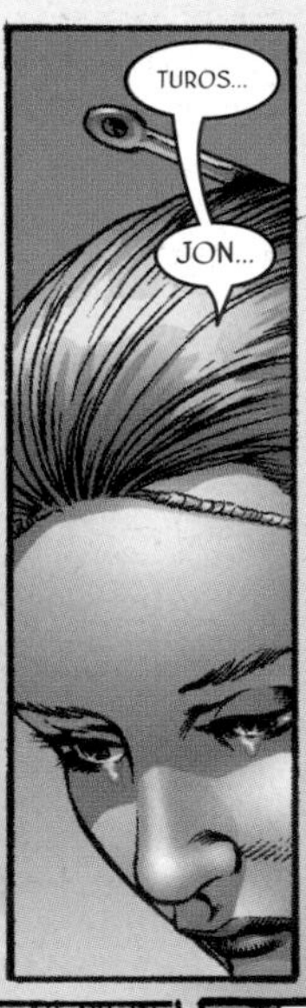

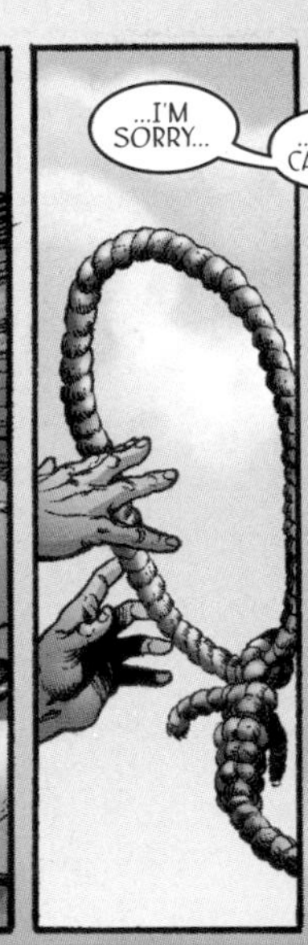

WHAT DO YOU DO, JON?
REVEAL TUROS NOW AND HE'S SHAMED BEFORE THE MINISTER...
...IF THEY'RE PARTED...
...GOING A DISTANCE STRENGTHENS THE HEART, RIGHT?
NEVER INTERFERE. THAT'S THE LESSON HERE.
SIGH

I'M SORRY, JON!
GOOD JOURNEY!

KEEP HER TIGHT TO THE ISLAND, NOW--
VERY GOOD.
IDERIA!
ILAHN.
YOU CHOSE TO STAY.
I APPLAUD YOUR CHOICE.
YOU GOT MY GIFT, I ASSUME?
GIFT?
NO, I--
ILAHN...
...I CAME BACK FOR HIM, NOT YOU.
TUROS.
YOU WOULD STAY FOR TUROS.
HOW IRONIC--
TUROS IS HIDING ON THAT SHIP FOR YOU.
Oh, NO!
IDERIA!
NO.
NO!

I WAS HOPING YOU'D CHANGE YOUR MIND.
I WON'T DO IT AGAIN, I PROMISE.

JON, WHERE IS HE?
ON THE FAR SIDE OF PANIC, BUT RECOVERING QUICKLY.
SEE FOR YOURSELF.

ZZZZZRT
IDERIA!

Oh, TUROS!
IDERIA!
HARD AWAY!

SO.

YOU MAY HAVE WON HER, TUROS...

...BUT ONLY FOR NOW.

LADY IDERIA, THERE'S A GIFT INSIDE!
GIFT?
AAAH--

JUST SOMETHING I HAD DELIVERED HERE.
EXCUSE ME--IT'S...WOMEN'S BUSINESS.

IT'S SO BEAUTIFUL!
YES, CLARY.
THANK YOU.

YOU'RE WELCOME!
KLEK
KLIK

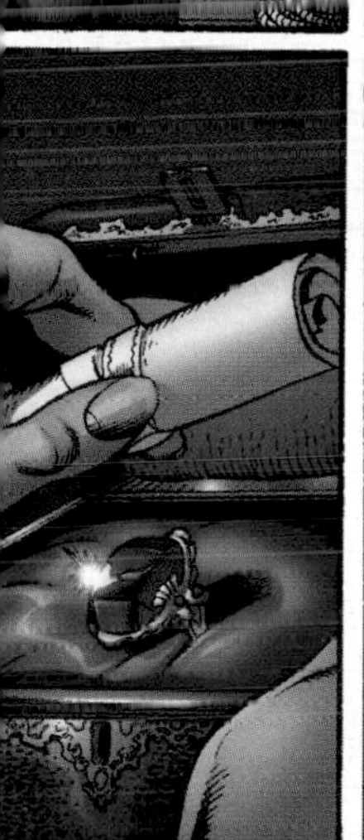

Ideria, please reconsider and return.
This gem is my promise to you--the world and more.

Do not underestimate my desire.

I will win you.
As a woman or a widow, you will be mine.
DAMN YOU, ILAHN!

MASTER ILAHN!
HERE FOR MORE PRIVATE ENTERTAINMENT?

NO.
THOSE MEN YOU TOLD ME YOU KNEW.
CONTACT THEM FOR ME AND I'LL SEE THAT YOUR SHOP'S DEBT TO MERIDIAN IS FORGIVEN.

IDERIA...THERE YOU ARE.
ARE YOU WELL?
JUST A LITTLE SICK, BUT IT'S PASSING FURTHER AWAY.
IDERIA, YOU RISKED YOUR LIFE TO BE HERE WITH ME...
...ARE YOU READY TO TAKE THE NEXT LEAP?
JON CAN MARRY US OUT HERE, IDERIA...
...*WILL* YOU?
Oh, TUROS!
--I--
I THINK WE SHOULD WA
UNTIL WE'RE BACK O
SOLID GROUND BEFO
MAKING THAT SERIOU
A DECISION.
SHHH...
I UNDERSTAND.
WE HAVE ALL THE TIME IN THE WORLD.
NO HURRY.
NO HEIR...
...IF THERE'S MUCH MORE DELAY.
YOUR GENEROSITY IS ASTOUNDING, MASTER ILAHN.
I'LL SEE TO IT RIGHT AWAY.
SEE THAT YOU DO.
SEND ME WORD AT THE MINISTER'S RESIDENCE.
YOU'VE CHOSEN UNWISELY, IDERIA, BUT I'LL MAKE THINGS *RIGHT*.

Mother caught the essence of Demelria in her work, the balance of beauty against the encroaching decay that makes us appreciate the beauty more...
...but there's a feeling of something more, something bad under the surface...
...as if the poisonous areas they crossed to reach the caverns had touched her personally.
But that's not likely...

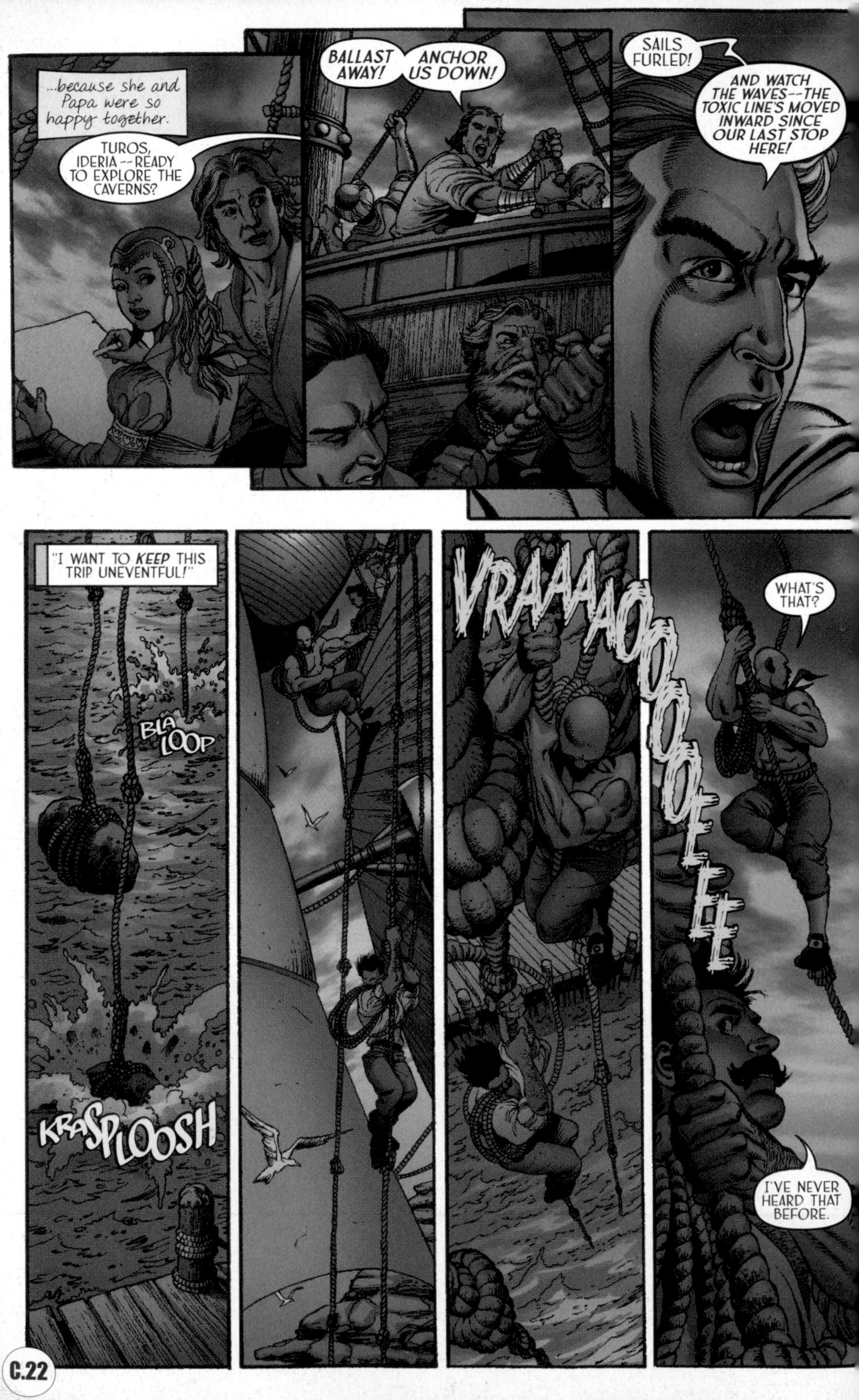

...because she and Papa were so happy together.

TUROS, IDERIA--READY TO EXPLORE THE CAVERNS?

BALLAST AWAY!

ANCHOR US DOWN!

SAILS FURLED!

AND WATCH THE WAVES--THE TOXIC LINE'S MOVED INWARD SINCE OUR LAST STOP HERE!

VRAAAAOOOOEEE
THAT'S
OT THE
VAVES?
NO, MA'AM. THAT'S SOMETHING ELSE.
QUIET, EVERYONE!
THERE'S SOMETHING NEW IN THESE WATERS?
THERE MAY BE. I'VE HEARD RUMORS--
ON!
THE WATER!
BLUUURBLE
WHAT IN THE NAME OF --
VRAAAAOOOOEEE
--ALL?!
AIIEEEEE!

VRAAAOOOEE
KRAAAK SKRUNNNCH
UNFURL THE SAILS!
KRNNNKH
HANG ON, LADY IDERIA!
YAAAAH!
KRNNNCHOOOM
THE SAILS!
WE'VE GOT TO CATCH THE WIND TO RISE!

WE'RE LOST, JON! THE CREATURE'S DONE US IN!
THE SAIL'S GONE! WITHOUT IT, WE'LL BE SHOT TO AIRLESS HEIGHTS!
KRERAAAK
NO! THIS SHIP'S NOT LOST!
RAAAAOOOEEE
WE JUST NEED AN ANCHOR TO DRAG US TO RIGHTS!
SPLUTCH

YOU'VE DONE IT, TUROS!
I'LL MAKE A SAILOR OF YOU YET!
SAILS AWAY!
ANCHOR SET!
SAILS!
ANCHOR SET!
SAILS SET!
TUROS! CUT YOUR LINE!
WHHKKT
SPLOOOSH

And Papa said their journey was nothing to boast about!
REPAIRS SHOULD DELAY US ONLY A WEEK OR TWO.
TAKE YOUR TIME IN THE CITY-- THERE'S NOT MUCH BEYOND THE MAIN STRIP, SO YOU'LL GET TO KNOW IT WELL.
I'LL STAY WITH THE SHIP.
Oh, AND TUROS?
I'M DOWN A HARPOON, O HUNTER OF BEASTS, SO YOU MIGHT WANT TO SEE IF ONE'S AVAILABLE FOR SALE.
JON, IF I COULD, I'D BUY YOU A NEW SHIP.
BUT THAT WOULDN'T GIVE YOU THE SAME SATISFACTION AS COMPLAINING OVER REPAIRS.
LADY IDERIA, WHAT ARE THEY DOING?
MINING, CLARY...
"...THIS IS WHERE THEY DIG OUT THE ORE THAT MAKES THE ISLANDS FLOAT."
THESE MEN ARE WORKING THEMSELVES TO DEATH...IT'S INHUMANE.
THEY'RE WORKING TO EARN THEIR SPOT IN THE SKY, TUROS.
LOOK AGAIN--

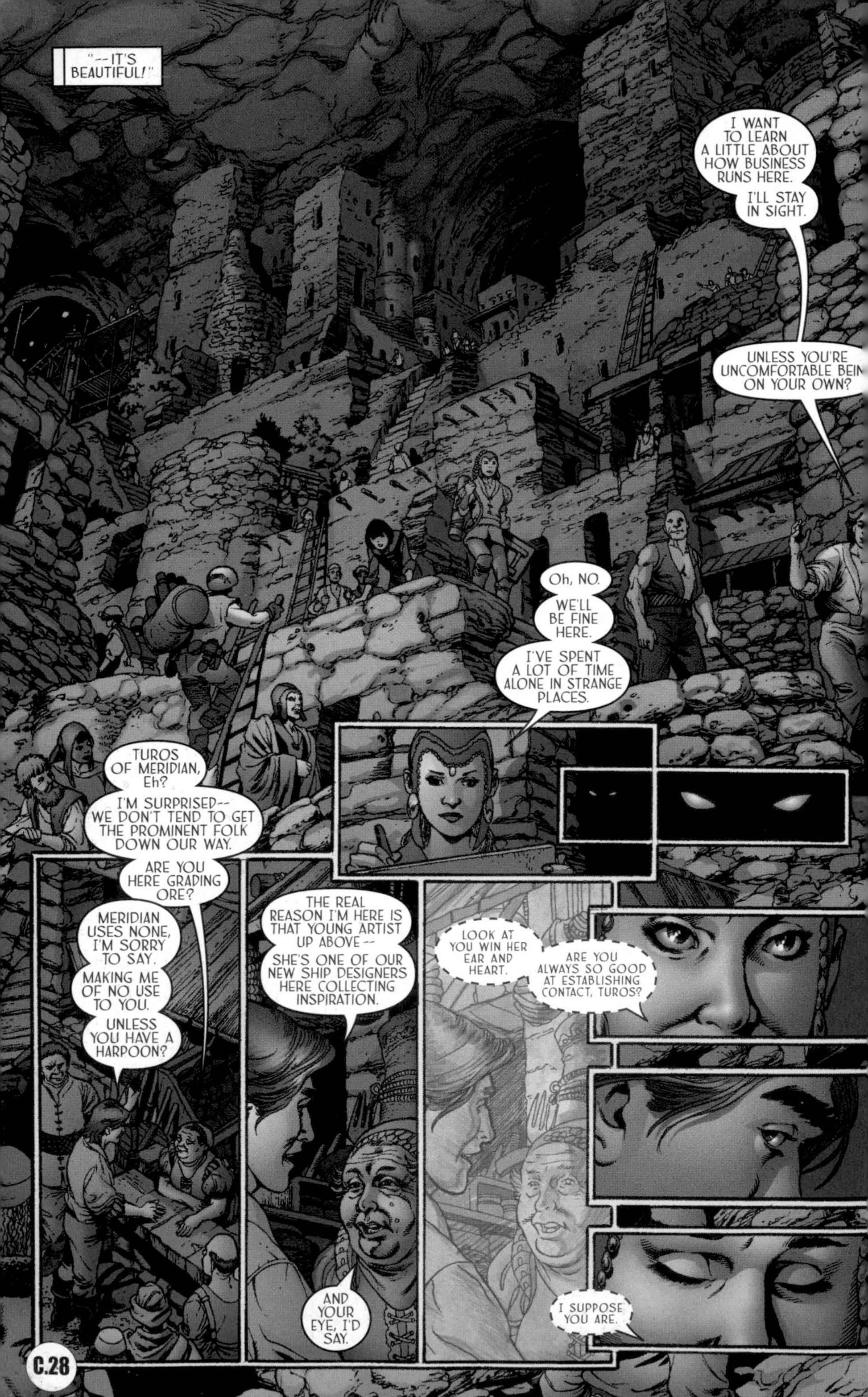
"--IT'S BEAUTIFUL!"
I WANT TO LEARN A LITTLE ABOUT HOW BUSINESS RUNS HERE.
I'LL STAY IN SIGHT.
UNLESS YOU'RE UNCOMFORTABLE BEIN ON YOUR OWN?
Oh, NO.
WE'LL BE FINE HERE.
I'VE SPENT A LOT OF TIME ALONE IN STRANGE PLACES.
TUROS OF MERIDIAN, Eh?
I'M SURPRISED-- WE DON'T TEND TO GET THE PROMINENT FOLK DOWN OUR WAY.
ARE YOU HERE GRADING ORE?
MERIDIAN USES NONE, I'M SORRY TO SAY.
MAKING ME OF NO USE TO YOU.
UNLESS YOU HAVE A HARPOON?
THE REAL REASON I'M HERE IS THAT YOUNG ARTIST UP ABOVE--
SHE'S ONE OF OUR NEW SHIP DESIGNERS HERE COLLECTING INSPIRATION.
AND YOUR EYE, I'D SAY.
LOOK AT YOU WIN HER EAR AND HEART.
ARE YOU ALWAYS SO GOOD AT ESTABLISHING CONTACT, TUROS?
I SUPPOSE YOU ARE.
C.28

THIS MAN WILL BRING TRUE CHANGE TO DEMETRIA?
THIS MAN WILL STRIVE TO BRING TOGETHER EARTH AND SKY...
...THOUGH HE WILL NOT BE THEIR LINK.
PATIENCE, GERES. HE WILL BUT PLANT THE SEED.
YOUR DREAMS WILL NOT BEAR FRUIT UNTIL THE NEXT GENERATION.
...AND PRAY I LIVE LONG ENOUGH TO SEE IT.
THEY'RE NEARLY HERE. LET'S GO TO MEET THEM.
SO YOU SEE THE MINERS AS EXPLOITED?
YES, BUT YOU COULD CHANGE THAT...
I CAN ONLY HOPE YOUR VISION SEES TRUE, MUSE...
THEY MUST BRING THE ARTIST, TOO.
IT'S BEEN ARRANGED.
...ALL YOU'D NEED IS A GUILD STRUCTURE LIKE OUR SHIPBUILDERS--
SHHH!
ACTUALLY, I'M A MESSENGER.
I'VE BEEN ASKED TO BRING YOU TO MEET SOMEONE SPECIAL.
COME WITH ME, PLEASE.
Oh?
MAY I ASK WHERE WE'RE BEING HUSTLED OFF TO?
IF YOU'RE LOOKING FOR RANSOM...
NO, NOT AT ALL!
FORGIVE ME!
MY FRIEND THE MUSE HAS ME SO ACCUSTOMED TO LIVING FOR THE FUTURE I SOMETIMES FORGET TO BRING CLARITY TO THE PRESENT!
COME FURTHER AND I'LL EXPLAIN.
Oh, MY!
WHA--?

WHAT IS THIS PLACE?
TUROS OF MERIDIAN, LADY IDERIA--
I WANT YOU TO UNDERSTAND THE FULL IMPORT OF MY WORDS. OUTSIDE OF THOSE OF US WHO RUN THE SHAM CITY ABOVE...
YOU TWO ARE THE FIRST OUTSIDERS WE'VE ALLOWED DOWN TO VIEW THE SECRET CITY.
I AM GERES, MINISTER OF ANHEIM.
THIS WAS OUR ANCESTORS' HOME, ALL BUT DESTROYED BY THE CATACLYSM.
WE ARE SLOWLY RECLAIMING IT FOR FUTURE GENERATIONS.
AFTER HUNDREDS OF YEARS, WE DRAW NEAR TO THE TIME WHEN WE CAN SHARE OUR SECRET TREASURE...
YOU'VE GOT GARDENS DOWN THERE!
ON *SURFACE* SOIL? DON'T THE TOXINS--?
THAT'S THE MIRACLE WE GUARD.
NEW STRAINS THAT BREAK DOWN AND NEUTRALIZE THE TOXINS.
WE'RE WILLING TO SHARE THEM, BUT WE WON'T LET THEM BE CONTROLLED AS COMMODITIES.
THAT'S WHY WE NEED YOU.
A MINISTER-TO-BE AND AN ARTIST?
WHAT CAN *WE* DO?
ONE THE HEART AND ONE THE VISION...
...FROM THEIR JOINING COMES THE DAUGHTER OF MERIDIAN TO--
DAUGHTER?
OURS?
SILENCE! THE MUSE OF GIATAN SPEAKS!
COMES THE CHILD BORN OF THE WIND WHO WILL WIELD FIRE TO JOIN EARTH AND SKY!
SO SEES THE EYES OF GIATAN!
MOTHER ALONE, OPEN YOUR EYES TO--
--THE CHIL YOU WILL B BUT NEVER K SHE IS NEEDE HAVE YOU T STRENGTH MAKE IT SO

SEE WITH ME!
KNOW IT TO BE TRUE!
OUR DAUGHTER...
I SEE.
BUT IF WE...
...ILAHN.
MINISTER GERES, THERE'S TROUBLE ABOVE!
IN THE CITY?
NO!
THEIR SHIP!
OUR SHIP?!
IDERIA, WE'VE GOT TO GO!
WAIT...
MINISTER GERES, KEEP THIS SAFE.
GIVE IT TO HER.
I...MAY NEVER KNOW HER...
...BUT I'D LIKE HER TO KNOW ME.

FWASHOOOM
FIRE AWAY, MEN! THEY WON'T TAKE OUR SHIP!
WATCH YOUR AIM-- WE DON'T WANT TO RISK THE NEW ONE IF WE CAN AVOID IT!
NO SHIP'S WORTH THE PRICE OF OUR LIVES, JON!
MERCENARIES?
BUT--WHY WOULD THEY WASTE TIME ON ONE OF *OUR* SHIPS?
WE CARRY NO WEALTH BUT THE VESSELS THEMSELVES!
MAYBE *SHIPS* ARE WHAT THEY WANT!
LAUNCH ME!
BUT MASTER TUROS, OUR ORDERS! WE CAN'T RISK *YOU!*
YOU WILL TAKE *MY* WORD OVER YOUR ORDERS!
DO IT!
Papa never knew who had sent those men...

...or why they'd chosen such a meager target.

They seemed intent on death, not just theft...

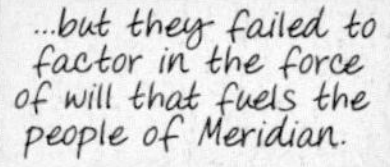
...but they failed to factor in the force of will that fuels the people of Meridian.

GET OFF MY SHIP!

YOU WORK FOR *HIM,* DON'T YOU?

ILAHN SENT YOU!

Papa said that was, in truth, his first day as Minister of Meridian...
...the first time he acted on his OWN authority.
He decided that if they wanted the new ship...
...they could HAVE it.
TUROS!
GET YOUR HANDS OFF HER!
Mother appeared to be very impressed by his newfound authority.

When she saw what he'd sacrificed for their safety...
THEY DIDN'T WANT THE SHIP...
WHAT DID THEY WANT?
...she no longer feared their future together.
IDERIA...
...PLEASE TELL ME NO ONE CAN KEEP US APART.
NO ONE CAN, TUROS.
MY ANSWER IS YES.
COME WHAT MAY.
Meanwhile, Ilahn had left Meridian for Cadador...
...where his own new bride awaited him.
MASTER ILAHN, IT IS MY JOY TO PRESENT MY DAUGHTER...
...CLAIRESSA.
CLAIRESSA?
AREN'T YOU PLEASED TO MEET MASTER ILAHN?
Oh...
...YES.
PLEASED.
LIKEWISE.

SHE WAS SO BEAUTIFUL...
...I WISH I'D KNOWN HER.
IT'S OBVIOUS SHE KNEW *YOU*.
I HAVE MY ROLE TO PLAY, CHILD. TO MY ENDS I MUST BE HERE AND THERE.
HERE I AM TO URGE YOU ON TOWARD YOUR DESTINY...
...*THERE* I WAS SO YOUR MOTHER...
SO THAT SHE WOULD BE HERE WITH ME.
WITH ME *ALWAYS*.
THANK YOU.

MERIDIAN • CHAPTER FOURTEEN

EMBOL!
WHAT ARE YOU DOING?
KILLING IT BEFORE IT CAN KILL US!
INGRA SAID WE WERE TO *OBSERVE* THE SIGIL-BEARERS, *NOT* ATTACK!
I DON'T CARE!
I'D RATHER RISK HER WRATH THAN DEATH AT THIS STRANGER'S TOUCH!
EMBOL, *NO!*
IF YOU HAVEN'T KILLED IT, IT WILL BE *ANGRY* NOW.
YOU NEED TO LEARN WHEN TO BE FORCEFUL, CHYIA. THE SURVIVORS ARE THOSE WHO KNOW WHEN TO STRIKE FIRST!

THIS... IS HARDLY THE WAY TO... NEGOTIATE.
I NEED-- *UNH*--TO KEEP **CONTROL**.
YOU PEOPLE-- *HNH!*-- NEED A LESSON IN... THE COURTESIES... OF EXCHANGE.
I SEE MY TASK CLEARLY...

...I AM TO BE YOUR ADVISOR IN THE WAYS OF *WILL!*

I CANNOT BE KILLED BECAUSE I WILL NOT *ALLOW* IT!
SEE HOW I DESTROY MY DEATH!

THE ENERGY HERE...

AAAAAH!
IT'S--
--SO--
--SO--
--PURE!

OW CAN HE--?
STEAL POWER FROM US?
THEY CAN *DO* THAT.
I ASSUMED, WITH ALL OF US, THERE'D BE NO TROUBLE RESTRAINING HIM, BUT--
SO, RHO RHUSTANE--YOU PLANNED TO BRING MINISTER ILAHN TO YOUR WORLD ALL ALONG.
WHAT IS THIS SUBSTANCE HE'S ABLE TO...FEED ON?
WHY CAN'T *I?*

YOUR GIFT COMES FROM ME, REESHA, NOT FROM TAPPING THE UNIVERSAL ENERGIES.
ONLY I CAN BESTOW YOUR FIRE.
AND I NEVER PLANNED--
PLAN?
YOU DIDN'T PLAN!
YOU DIDN'T THINK!
YOU'RE ALWAYS DOING THIS, RHORF! ALWAYS RUNNING OFF HALF-COCKED, GETTING EVERYBODY ALL EXCITED!
NOW LOOK WHAT YOU'VE DONE!
IF ONLY YOU'D THINKGGGKK
EGYUUURK!
NOW WOULD BE A GOOD TIME TO UNHAND ME, ENTUGRO!
NOW?
REESHA, STAND CLEAR!
I MAY NEED TO RETRIEVE THAT WHICH I GAVE YOU TO--URK! --SURVIVE THIS!

IT'S GOOD--
--GOOD.
FLOODING THROUGH--
NO.
THIS HUNGER... ADDICTION...
I WILL NOT SLIP AGAIN...
I WILL NOT...
...BE...
...CONTROLLED...
YOU ARE FILLING ME WITH LIMITLESS POWER--
--WITH THIS FIRE, I CAN SURPASS GODS!

NO CRAVING...
...NO POWER...
...WILL BE...
...MY MASTER!
Ah.
BETTER.
ELYSIA IS A FASCINATING PLACE, RHO RHUSTANE.
GET UP.
I BELIEVE YOU AND I HAVE MUCH TO DISCUSS.

...LIKE WHY YOU SEEM SO DETERMINED TO *PUSH* ME THIS WAY.
I DO THANK YOU FOR SEEING THAT I GOT THIS GIFT FROM MY MOTHER, BUT...
...WHY ARE YOU *HERE?*
I WILL COME WHEN NEEDED, IN THE FORM MOST FITTING.
I AM THE EYES WHO SEE WHAT COMES AND I MUST MAKE YOU READY.
READY FOR WHAT?
WHEN THE TWO SIDES MUST JOIN AS ONE AGAINST THE REVERSAL AND ENDING.
WHA--?
YOU DON'T MEAN I'LL BE WORKING *WITH* UNCLE ILAHN?
The Muse of Giatan is a very strange creature.
MUSE...?
As surprising as it was to find her suddenly gone, it had been more so to discover HER in the secret caverns of Anheim bearing a case of my mother's artwork and stories of knowing her...
WHY?
There was clearly some greater mystery involved.
I'm not certain I'll ever know her true purpose...

...and I'm not sure it matters.
I did want to ask her more questions that night, but with what I'd learned about what my parents had done there...
...my head already held enough.
Time to let thoughts rest and sort themselves out.
I was in a place of ancient mysteries that held new secrets...
...AND being followed by someone who'd never trailed shy deer through the woods.
If I'd learned not to be taken by surprise...
...I'd also learned...
...to be the surprise!
YAAAH!

RENNER!
SEPHIE!
Oh!
I DIDN'T MEAN TO BE FOLLOWING *YOU*...
WHO DID YOU THINK I WAS?
I--I SAW THE LIGHT AT THE STOREHOUSE AND--
--SINCE THERE ARE STRANGERS IN ANHEIM--
--NOT THAT I THINK ANY OF YOU WOULD--!
THE STOREHOUSE IS MY RESPONSIBILITY. I COULDN'T JUST *ASSUME* WHOEVER WAS UP HERE HAD GOOD INTENTIONS...
WHAT WE HAVE HERE ISN'T UABLE IN THE USUAL SENSE, BUT IT'S IRREPLACEABLE.
WOULD U LIKE TO EE WHAT M TALKING ABOUT?
THAT WOULD BE NICE.
YOU MIGHT THINK IT'S JUST *SEEDS*, BUT SOMEONE FROM LONG AGO GATHERED AND STORED A SAMPLE OF *EVERYTHING* THAT GROWS ON DEMETRIA!
I'VE BEEN WORKING MY WAY THROUGH, CHECKING FOR VIABILITY, NOT ONLY TO BRING STRAINS BACK...
...I HOPE THIS DOESN'T SOUND STUPID...
...BUT TO HONOR THE PERSON WHO WORKED SO HARD TO SAVE THEM.
THAT'S NOT STUPID. THAT'S THOUGHTFUL.
SOME ARE RUINED, LIKE THESE--
--LOST FOR ALL TIME BECAUSE OF A FAULTY SEAL.

WAIT...
...MAYBE NOT FOR *ALL* TIME!

HERE YOU ARE.
SEPHIE!
WHAT ARE YOU!
HOW COULD YOU--?
LET ME REPHRASE THAT. WHAT YOU ARE IS WONDERFUL.
THANK YOU--YOU'VE JUST DONE A MIRACULOUS THING.
HAVE YOU ALWAYS BEEN SO...
...SPECIAL?
I'M...STILL LEARNING WHAT I CAN DO.
MY ABILITY TO...FIX...THINGS COMES FROM THE MARK ON MY HEAD.
IT'S ALL HAPPENING SO QUICKLY...
TOO QUICKLY, CRENNER.
I'M SORRY, BUT...THERE'S SOMEONE...
...BACK HOME ON MERIDIAN...
...HIS NAME IS JAD.

KNNNNNT
KNNNNNT
KZZZZZT
KRAAK
KSHOOM
KRASHOOM
SHOOM
JAD, NO!
IT'S TIME TO TAKE COVER!
BUT THE SHIP!

"IT ISN'T WORTH YOUR LIFE! NO THING IS!"
KRA KA KOOM

KRAAAAKK

THAT WAS CLOSE.
SOMETHING WE HAVE TO LEARN TO LIVE WITH HERE, MEIER.
DAD -- WHAT'S *THAT*?

I DON'T KNOW, SON.
IN ALL MY YEARS -- THAT'S A PHENOMENON I'VE NEVER SEEN.
BUT...
...INSIDE...
...CAN YOU SEE --?

"-- IT'S NOT JUST A FREAK OF THE WEATHER...IT'S... IT'S A *PERSON!*"

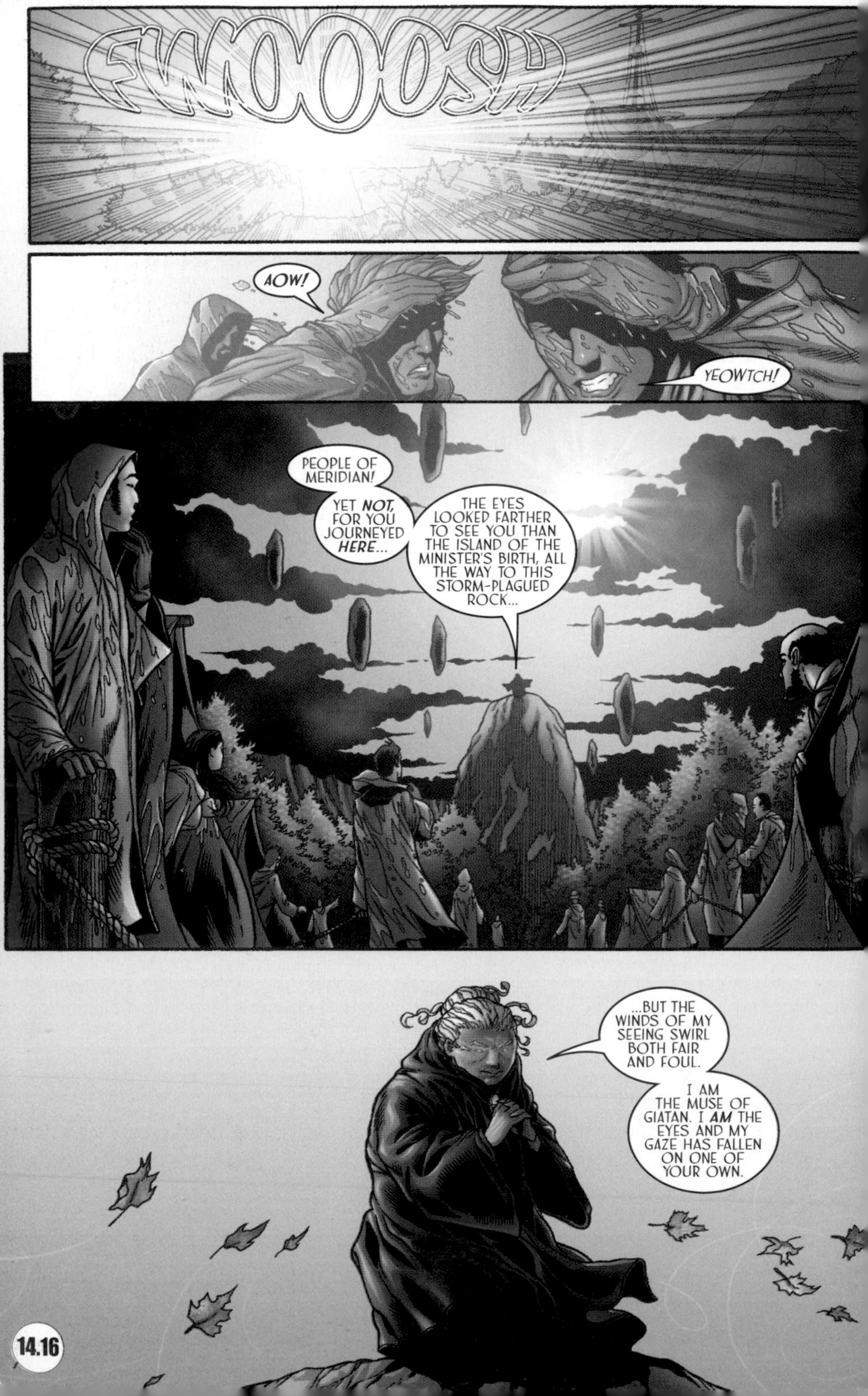

AOW!

YEOWTCH!

PEOPLE OF MERIDIAN!

YET *NOT*, FOR YOU JOURNEYED *HERE*...

THE EYES LOOKED FARTHER TO SEE YOU THAN THE ISLAND OF THE MINISTER'S BIRTH, ALL THE WAY TO THIS STORM-PLAGUED ROCK...

I NEVER THOUGHT I'D SEE THE DAY DEREN BEQ WOULD COME OUT OF HER LAIR AND JOURNEY DOWN TO ANHEIM WITH US.
FUNNY MAN, CEREG.
YOU AND DREN CAN COME WORK THE LAIR'S CROWD SOMETIME.
I HAVEN'T CHANGED A THING.
I STILL DON'T WANT TO BE A PART OF THE HOLIER-THAN-THOU MISSION THAT CONSUMES YOUR LIVES DOWN HERE...
...BUT I'VE GOT SOMETHING I'VE GOT TO MAKE RIGHT.
I'M GLAD YOU CHANGED YOUR MIND ABOUT US, DEREN.
NEXT THING WE KNOW, YOU'LL BE TENDING THE GARDENS--BEATING THE CROPS INTO BLOOM!
I MISUSED SEPHIE AND I NEED TO APOLOGIZE.
THEN I CAN GET BACK TO MINDING MY OWN BUSINESS.

SEPHIE, ALTHOUGH I REGRET YOU ARE LEAVING US SO SOON, WE HAVE SOMETHING WE'D LIKE YOU TO TAKE WITH YOU ON YOUR JOURNEY.
BESIDES ME.
I MEAN, I WANT TO COME WITH YOU.
IF IT'S ALL RIGHT WITH MINISTER GERES, OF COURSE.
WHICH MEANS I HAVE TO GO TO KEEP YOU OUT OF TROUBLE... OR YOUR GRANDPA WILL MULCH ME INTO THE GARDENS.
I HAVE NO IDEA IF I'LL BE SUCCESSFUL IN CONVINCING ANY OF THE CITIES TO OPENLY DEFY ILAHN--
YOU WILL.
JUST PULL A STUNT LIKE YOU DID OUTSIDE THE LAIR.
YOU?
ONCE THEY SEE YOU FLY AND TOSS THEM LIKE CUSHIONS, THEY'LL DO ANYTHING YOU ASK.
YOU--
YOU!
YOU DIDN'T HAVE TO HAVE THEM KIDNAP ME!
YOU COULD HAVE JUST ASKED.
GROW UP.
I DON'T ASK.
I DECIDE.

AND WHAT I'VE DECIDED TO DO IS *HELP* YOU.
I'VE STARTED *SPREADING* THE STORY OF WHAT YOU'RE UP TO. THE TALE'S ALREADY ON ITS WAY OUT OF THE CAVERNS AND OFF TO THE LANDS AND THE ISLANDS.
IT'LL BE THERE BEFORE YOU ARE.

THANK YOU, I THINK.
I HOPE THAT'S A GOOD IDEA.
OF COURSE IT'S A GOOD IDEA.
I'VE USED UP ALL MY BAD ONES ALREADY.

LADIES, WE'RE HERE.
MANY YEARS AGO, WHEN YOUR FATHER TRIED TO UNITE US ALL, HE HAD A SYMBOL CREATED.

SOMETHING TO *SIGNIFY* THE UNITY HE WAS TRYING TO ACHIEVE.
WE MODIFIED IT A LITTLE TO SUIT YOU...
...WE GAVE IT YOUR MARK.

BY THE STARS--
MINISTER *GERES!*

"IT'S THE MOST BEAUTIFUL SHIP I'VE EVER SEEN!"
Once, when I was looking through Jon's logbooks, I ran across a sketch for a ship like this.
I asked if it had ever been built.
ONCE, he said.
GERES, FIND SOMEBODY TO MIND THE LAIR FOR ME.
I'M GOING.
I'M PLEASED.
IF ANYONE CAN HELP SEPHIE MANEUVER THROUGH THE WORLD, DEREN...
...IT'S *YOU*.

YOU HAVE OUR BEST WISHES, MINISTER OF MERIDIAN, AND MY GRANDSON'S ADDITION TO YOUR CAUSE IS PROOF OF OUR SUPPORT.
SHOULD YOU NEED ANYTHING MORE--
YOU'VE DONE MORE THAN ENOUGH, MINISTER GERES.
NOW IT'S MY TURN.
WHATEVER GAVE ME THIS SIGIL MADE ME THE ONE PERSON WHO CAN STOP MY UNCLE.
THAT'S WHAT I HAVE TO DO.
SWIFT WINDS AND GOOD JOURNEY, SEPHIE!
THANK YOU!
Less than two weeks ago, I was a little girl who fell from the sky.
Now I was Minister of Meridian, Captain of my parents' ship, able to fly, to heal, to fight... definitely no longer the same little girl...
There was no turning back on this journey.

They'd only made this ship once, Jon said, and it was lost -- it didn't serve its purpose.
I'd always assumed he meant it wouldn't maneuver correctly...
...but now I realize it was the mission that failed, not the design.
Here we were, off on a second try and I carried along the dream of my parents even as their ship carried me.
With their help, I would succeed.
All I had to do was find allies and unite them.
Change the whole world!
...then bring llahn down.